Warbonnet Creek

Trouble is looming along Warbonnet Creek between a powerful rancher named Marryat and the smaller cattlemen. Ned Hogan and his neighbours, the Caseys, are leading the opposition but they are up against Marryat's hired gunmen and corrupt Sheriff Templeman, leaving them with no protection from the law.

With his ranch house set on fire and a murderous rifleman hunting him, Hogan is forced to go into hiding. Who is this mysterious stranger and whom is he working for? Now Hogan must step outside the law before the killing ends and peace can return.

Warbonnet Creek

Greg Mitchell

A Black Horse Western

ROBERT HALE · LONDON

Typeset by Derek Doyle & Associates, Shaw Heath
Printed and bound in Great Britain by
Antony Rowe Limited, Wiltshire

ONE

Walter Hill probably never saw the man who killed him. The heavy bullet, fired from ambush, hit him squarely in the center of the chest and knocked him back over the rump of his startled horse. The killer knew that his aim had been true, and he did not approach his victim.

Ned Hogan was saddling his horse prior to checking on his cattle when he heard the distant report of a heavy rifle. It differed from the flat sound of the Winchester .44/40, which most ranchers owned. Someone hunting, he told himself and thought no more about it until he heard a galloping horse on the hard-packed clay road that ran past his Rocking H ranch. He looked up to see a riderless pinto horse galloping toward him. He recognized it as one that belonged to his neighbor and hurried through the gate to stand in the horse's path. The animal saw the man and slowed down. As Hogan extended his arms, it skidded to a stop.

Speaking gently, he caught the horse's bridle. The reins were knotted together, unlike the unjoined reins favored by working cowmen. They had fallen behind the saddle horn and remained there. Hill had arthritic hands and habitually knotted his reins together in case he should accidentally drop one.

'You old devil,' Hogan told the pinto. 'You've taken off and left Walter to walk home. Took fright when he fired that shot, I suppose.'

Still unsuspecting, he collected his own mount and led the pinto back along the trail. He was sure that he would find his neighbor cursing the runaway. Or he was until he came over a slight ridge and saw a still body on the ground in the distance. He had seen the awkward sprawl of a dead man before. Thoroughly alarmed, he urged his gray gelding into a canter, although instinct told him that it would not matter if he got there a few seconds later.

As he dismounted beside the corpse he saw that there was nothing he could do. He turned the dead man over, and noticed a large exit wound in his back. The bullet had passed right through him.

The only cover for the shooter was a clump of bushes about fifty yards away, and Hogan's hand strayed to his hip where he usually carried a Colt .45. Too late he remembered that he had left the weapon in his ranch house. For all he knew, the killer could still be lurking there, seeking another victim.

He plucked the dead man's old Remington .44 from the holster and immediately stepped behind the sheltering bulk of his horse. But no shot came and after a while he knew that the murderer had left the scene.

Walter Hill returned to his ranch tied across his horse with his own lariat. His two hands, George Hynes and Ed Corbett were replacing a broken corral rail but came running when they saw the pinto with its grim burden.

Hynes got there first. 'It's the boss. What happened?'

'I heard the shot and saw his horse coming down the road. When I went looking I found him dead on the trail. Somebody ambushed him,' Hogan explained as he dismounted.

Together the three men carried the body to the ranch house veranda.

'Any sign of who did it?' Corbett asked. He was a thin, stooped man who had worked on Hill's ranch for several years.

'I didn't hang around as I didn't have my gun with me and was not too keen on taking on a rifle with Walter's old six-shooter. I'll go back to my ranch and get one and I'll bring back Juán Perez. We'll see if we can find any tracks. It might be best if you fellows did what you could for Walter, and someone will need to ride to town and notify Sheriff Templeman.'

Corbett growled. 'That useless sonofabitch won't be much help. He won't do anything for us small ranchers. Marryat has him in his pocket.'

Marryat owned the largest ranch in Warbonnet Creek and also ran the most stock on the open range. All the valley's ranchers had stock that they grazed together on the open range.

'Marryat's always accusing us of being rustlers,' Hynes said angrily. He was young and had little time for the district's biggest rancher. 'The boss reckoned he was behind that note he got the other day.'

Hogan asked: 'What note?'

'It was in the mailbox,' Corbett explained. 'Said that Walter was a rustler and told him to get out of the valley. Walter thought it was just someone trying to scare him. It wasn't signed or even in an envelope.'

'Looks like somebody really had it in for

him,' Hogan said as he remounted. 'I'll pass the word to the Caseys and be back here soon with Perez.'

Juán Perez was a wiry young man, half-Mexican, half-Indian. He had worked for Hogan for two years and had proved himself to be a top ranch hand. Though some of his neighbours did not trust half-breeds of any kind, Hogan had always found him to be very reliable. He was the rancher's only permanent hand, although he would employ a couple more at round-up time.

Perez was saddling a horse to go looking for him when the rancher rode up. 'I was just going looking for you, Ned. I saw you take off up the road with Walter's horse. What's happening?'

'Someone murdered Walter. I found him shot on the trail. I've just come home to get my gun. I'll ride over and tell the Caseys. Be ready to ride in half an hour. We'll see then if we can pick up any tracks.' With those few words Hogan hurried inside and returned buckling on his gun belt. He mounted quickly, wheeled his horse, touched it lightly with the spurs and headed for the neighbouring ranch.

Casey's dogs were barking long before he reached the house. A female figure appeared at the door and Hogan hoped that it was Ellie

Casey, but as he rode closer he saw that it was her mother, Jean. The older woman smiled as she saw the young rancher.

'What brings you here in such a hurry, Ned?'

'There's been a murder, Jean. Someone shot Walter Hill.'

'That's awful. Do you know who did it?'

'Not yet but I'm going to where he was shot with Juán. If anyone can pick up the tracks he can. Is Mike about?'

'What's this about a murder?' Ellie Casey appeared at the door. Her apron and hands were covered in flour but Hogan still thought that she was the most beautiful girl he had ever seen. The curly, light-brown hair and sparkling blue eyes always seemed to set his heart jumping.

'Howdy, Ellie. I was just telling your mother that Walter Hill has been murdered. I found him shot on the trail. He never knew what hit him.'

'That's terrible. Mr Hill was such a nice man.'

'Someone didn't think so,' her mother said. Turning to Ellie she asked: 'Where did your father say he was going with the boys?'

'He said they were going to push any cattle out of Swampy Canyon; the water's drying up there and the feed isn't much good anyway.

Then they were going along the ridges to see if any cattle were drifting into the badlands. I could ride out and find them.'

'It might be best if you don't,' Hogan told her. 'We don't know what sort of person is running around out there. It's best that you stay on your guard here. When Mike and the boys come back you can tell them what's happened. When I find out more I'll let you know.'

He rode the mile and a half back to his own ranch where Perez was waiting with two horses. 'You might want to change horses, Ned. Old Barney that you're riding is getting on a bit. This bay horse might be better for a hard day.'

Perez was right but Hogan begrudged the time spent changing his saddle and fixing a Winchester carbine in a leather boot to it. He wanted to be after Hill's killer before the trail was too cold. He mounted quickly and the pair spurred for Hill's ranch.

They found Corbett waiting for them at the front gate. He too was wearing a six-gun and had a rifle on his saddle. 'George has gone for the sheriff and there was nothing I could do for Walter, so I put him inside and will be riding with you.'

'The more the merrier,' Hogan said. 'I couldn't get Mike Casey or his two boys.'

The big patch of blood, like a dark shadow on the ground, clearly showed where Hill had fallen. Nothing was to be gained by studying that and Perez took the lead as they approached the bushes from where the killer had fired. He dismounted, passed his reins to Hogan and went forward carefully on foot.

'He was lying up here, sighting his rifle through this bush,' the half-breed called to them. 'The ground's scuffed about but it's too hard to hold a decent track. My best bet is to see if I can find where he left his horse.'

Fifty yards away they found an erosion gully and saw where a horse had been tied there out of sight.

Perez shook his head. 'He had a horse probably around the fifteen-hand mark. Its near hind hoof is slightly more triangular than it should be, but that's common. Let's see if we can find where it went.'

They followed the tracks until they came to the main road to the town of Muddy Creek ten miles further to the north. There the prints left by horses, wagons and cattle made tracking impossible.

They rode up both sides of the road for a couple of miles but found nothing new.

Hogan told the others: 'Looks like he got

clear away and we can't even tell which way he went.'

'Riders coming.' Corbett pointed down the road, then said in surprise: 'Well I'll be danged. It's George and Sheriff Templeman.'

TWO

There was no mistaking the sheriff. Everything about him was for show, from his big palomino horse to the pearl-handled Schofield revolver on his hip. The man himself was large and imposing, with slightly greying hair, a handsome face and an imperious manner. The expression on his face as he approached indicated that he was not pleased to see the men from Warbonnet Creek.

'I met the sheriff half-way along the road,' Hynes explained. 'He was on his way out to see us.'

'I'm looking for you, Hogan,' the sheriff said.

'Looks like your search is over, Sheriff. But for once I'm pleased to see you. No doubt George told you about the murder.'

'He did. But I've also received a complaint about you. Mr Marryat said that you threatened him.'

'I just told him that the next time he calls me a rustler I'm going to knock his teeth down his lying throat, but right now I reckon murder is a bit more important than Marryat's cattle.'

Templeman disagreed. 'Marryat received a note yesterday telling him he would be killed if he didn't sell up and get out of the area. He thinks you sent it.'

'Like hell I did. My neighbour, Walter Hill got a similar note, too. Didn't George tell you that? Walter's dead now but I can assure you that I don't go around shooting my friends.' Hogan picked up his reins and said to Perez: 'Time we were going home, Juán. Sheriff Templeman will take over now. If you want a statement from me, Sheriff, you know where to find me.'

The riders were nearly home when they met Mike Casey and his eldest son, Tom. Both wore revolvers and had carbines on their saddles.

'I heard about Walter,' the older Casey said by way of greeting. 'Did you find any sign of who killed him?'

'Nothing really, Mike. We lost the killer's horse-tracks on the town road. There was a fair bit of traffic and we couldn't tell which way he went. Templeman has arrived now so I've left it to him.'

Tom Casey snorted. 'Templeman couldn't

15

track an elephant in snow if its trunk was bleeding. He won't find anything. How did he get on the scene so quick?'

Hogan laughed. 'He was coming to see me about my exchanging pleasantries with Marryat. Now he has a bit of real work to do, he'll get out of here as fast as he can.'

'We saw Marryat this morning,' Casey said seriously. 'He had Ace Collins with him. He reckoned that someone sent him a note threatening his life.'

Hogan frowned. Ace Collins was fast gaining a reputation as a gunfighter. He had killed a man in Muddy Creek only recently. Sheriff Templeman had been over-eager to see the killing as self-defence and rumour was that he was afraid to go against Collins. 'I wonder if Collins had anything to do with Hill's murder.'

'It's the sort of job he's always looking for,' Casey said. 'But he was too far away from where Hill was shot. It couldn't have been him.'

They rode back together. The Caseys declined the offer of a cup of coffee at Hogan's and continued down the road.

Later that afternoon Hogan and Perez took a horn-saw and rode out onto the range seeking one of their cows that had a horn turning in towards its eye. Luckily she was a distinctive light roan and was easy to see among the other range cattle. It took a while to find the cow but eventually they sighted her.

'There she is,' Perez said as he unfastened his lariat. 'I'll take the hindlegs.'

That arrangement suited Hogan because the half-breed was a master at throwing a heel catch.

When she saw the riders approaching the cow took off, but she was no match for the horses. Hogan roped her around the neck and his horse sat back on its haunches while he dallied the rope around the saddle horn. The cow swung sideways but did not fall. As it struggled, Perez flicked his rope around both heels with an underhand throw and took up the slack. The cow fell on her side and the taut ropes held her stretched out on the ground. Hogan took the horn-saw from his saddle and hurried to the fallen animal. The horn was within half an inch of the cow's eye and in time would have grown into it. Kneeling on her neck, Hogan worked quickly and cut off the tip of the horn so that the problem was fixed. He knew that the cow would not be feeling particularly grateful about the rough handling, so he removed the ropes cautiously and backed to where his horse stood waiting. He mounted just in time to avoid the charge that the animal made as soon as she regained her feet. The horse jumped sideways and the cow snorted, shook her head and trotted back to the rest of the grazing stock.

Cattle of many brands were running together and would continue to do so until the fall round-up. Many of the cows had calves at foot and as he rode by one bunch, Hogan saw a calf wearing his brand. He checked his horse because he knew that he had not branded it. Another surprise awaited him when he saw that the mother cow wore Marryat's brand.

'Look here, Juán,' he called. 'Someone's put my brand on one of Marryat's calves. What in hell is going on around here?'

'That is bad. It makes you look like a rustler. Some of the other ranchers have probably seen that calf already. This will be bad for your reputation and it will give Templeman an excuse to arrest you for rustling. What are you going to do now?'

'There's only one thing I can do. I have to see Marryat. Much as I dislike him I'll have to come to some sort of arrangement about it. We'll go there now. I think someone has set me up. That cow was a very distinctive colour and would be easy to spot later. Let's look at a few more odd-coloured ones on the way to Marryat's.'

The Marryat ranch was actually over a range of hills from Warbonnet Creek. On the ride there Hogan and Perez discovered three more distinctively coloured cows with calves wearing the Rocking H brand.

It was late in the afternoon when they arrived at Marryat's front gate. The big, sprawling ranch house with its barn and corrals was set back about half a mile from the entrance.

'Marryat gets a good view of any visitors,' Perez observed.

They were fifty yards from the buildings when the slight figure of the rancher appeared on the veranda. A larger man stood beside him. There was no mistaking Ace Collins. He was above medium height with a big nose and narrow eyes. He wore a neatly trimmed moustache and clothes that were too clean for a working cowhand. In an area where most men carried one gun, which they used rarely, Collins wore two. He was scowling as he recognized the visitor.

Marryat's greeting was far from friendly. 'What are you doing here, Hogan?' His voice was nervous.

'I just found some calves that someone had been using a running-iron on. It was my brand but the cows were yours. I don't know who did

19

it but it wasn't me.'

'I'm damn sure I wouldn't give away my calves. You're the only one who would profit from such a deal, Hogan.'

'I don't see any advantage in that sort of deal. I think someone is trying to set me up as a rustler. The cows are all easy to see and a rustler normally would not be that stupid. None of the calves I saw will be weaned by round-up time and I won't dispute their ownership but if that doesn't suit you we could always rope them on the open range and brand a bar through my brand. I know that open-range branding is not popular because it encourages rustling but this is a special case and I'll do things any way that suits you.'

The little rancher glared at Hogan. 'I don't know what your game is, Hogan, but I've reported your threats to Sheriff Templeman and you don't frighten me by sending me notes.'

'Let's get this straight, Marryat. I would not send you threatening notes. But you are not the only rancher to get one. Walter Hill got one of those notes and I found him murdered on the trail this morning.'

Marryat looked shocked. 'What happened?'

'Someone shot him from ambush. I heard the shot. Templeman is making enquiries at the ranch now. I doubt if he'll get anywhere, though.'

'I'll let you know about those calves,' Marryat said coldly as he turned to leave. 'Ace, please escort these men off my land.'

The gunfighter smiled. 'With pleasure, Mr Marryat.'

Collins hurried to a saddled horse that was hitched in the shade at the end of the veranda and scowled when he saw that the visitors had not waited for him. Angrily he threw himself into the saddle and cantered after them. When he caught up he hauled his mount back to a walk. 'Just making sure that you pair of rustlers don't steal the gate on the way out,' he sneered.

He received no reply.

The gate was sagging on its hinges and was much safer to open dismounted. Hogan stepped down and went as though to open it. Collins was enjoying the situation. He sat relaxed on his horse, convinced that he had intimidated the pair. He was not worried that Hogan was standing close to him. He should have been.

Hogan moved like lightning, catching the gunman's belt with one hand, and with the other whipping off his hat to swat the horse in the face. As his startled horse jumped away

Collins was dragged from his saddle. He landed on his back on the ground. A fist smashed against his jaw before he fully realized what had happened. Instinctively he groped for a gun but the double click of a cocked hammer told him that he was too late.

'Reach for a gun and you're dead.'

Collins had recovered enough to see that he was looking at the bore of Hogan's gun. Very carefully he kept his hands clear of his weapons.

'Unbuckle your gun belt.'

The man on the ground had no choice. Very carefully he undid the buckle.

'Now stand up.'

Collins came up off the ground, leaving his guns behind. Hogan motioned with his Colt. 'Step away from your guns.'

The angry gunfighter did as he was told.

Hogan kicked the gun belt out under the fence. Then he passed his own weapon to Perez. 'Kill him if he draws any sort of weapon. No man calls me a thief and a rustler, Collins. Now we'll see how tough you are when you're not hiding behind a pair of guns.'

The gunman did not hesitate. He charged in and ran into a straight left that jolted back his head and cut his lips. Stung and angry, he threw another wild punch but Hogan blocked it and hooked him over his guard. The punch clipped the gunfighter's chin, snapping his head sideways and leaving him glassy-eyed and swaying on his feet. The few punches the gunman threw were only vain attempts to escape the relentless attack and were either evaded or easily blocked. Mentally Collins was already defeated. He knew that he was in a contest that he could not win, and whatever fight was in him rapidly diminished. Hogan went after him with another left followed by a right cross. Collins went straight down. He lay there unmoving.

'You're not hurt that much,' Hogan muttered savagely. 'Get up and make a fight of it.'

The fallen man stirred and looked for a second as though he might rise. But then he groaned and fell back, utterly defeated. He knew what awaited him if he stood up.

Perez laughed. 'The only way this fight will go on, Ned, is if you lie down alongside that yeller coyote and hit him from there.'

Hogan picked up the gun belt and mounted his horse. 'I'll leave these down the trail for you.'

Perez passed him back his own gun and they left the Marryat ranch in their dust.

'I thought that Collins would be a bit tougher than that,' the half-breed said.

'So did I, but an old sheriff told me once that professional gunmen often are not good fist-fighters. They try to settle everything with a gun. They don't get into too many bare-knuckle fights in case they break their hands. Without their guns he reckoned a lot of them were easy meat. It was certainly true in this case.'

'You picked a dangerous way to test that notion,' Perez said. 'A coward can still be a bad enemy.'

THREE

Hogan was not surprised to find a note in his mailbox. It was the morning of Hill's funeral. Though it was not the day for his weekly mail delivery, he was sure that he was on somebody's list and had started daily checks of the mailbox. The note read: *Rustler. Move or you are next.*

He called Perez and they checked the hoofprints around the box. Again they lost the tracks, which had been covered by those of range cattle coming in to water at the creek.

Perez said: 'This coyote is pretty smart. I reckon he's done this before. He's riding a barefoot horse this time.'

'Maybe he's not as smart as he thinks,' Hogan said. 'Riding two different horses indicates that he is on a ranch with a good supply of horses, and the fact that this one is unshod means that he hasn't travelled far. I reckon

25

he's hiding around here somewhere.'

'That's probably right, but you be careful,' Perez warned. 'We know that he has a long-range rifle. This *hombre* knows his business.'

The ranchers from along Warbonnet Creek all attended the funeral. Hill was a bachelor and they speculated about what would happen with his ranch.

Nick Meyers, the only lawyer in the district, was able to answer that question. As executor of Hill's estate he had arranged the funeral. The dead man had a brother living in the East and he had inherited the ranch. The lawyer told them that the new owner had wanted the ranch sold. The two hands would remain to run the place until another owner took over. Meyers would pay their wages and recoup them from the estate after its sale.

'It's a wonder that Marryat hasn't put in an offer already,' Mike Casey suggested to the lawyer. He was fishing for information.

Poker-faced, Meyers answered carefully. 'It is a bit soon to know who will be making offers. I have not advertised the sale yet.' Any information he had would not be given away.

Hogan was looking among the mourners for Ellie Casey. He found her talking to another young man who was a stranger to him. They seemed to be enjoying each other's company and he felt a twinge of jealousy.

Ellie saw him and said: 'Ned, come over and meet our new neighbour.'

She introduced the young man as Sam Hockley. He shook hands and said that he had purchased a small ranch on the other side of Casey's a month previously. His hired hand had moved in earlier but Hockley himself had only been in the valley for about a week.

'You might have picked a bad time to buy a ranch around here,' Hogan told him.

Hockley looked concerned. 'So it seems. I certainly don't want to be involved in a range war. From what I hear, small ranchers like us are not very popular in some quarters.'

'You're right there,' Hogan told him. 'But this is a strange sort of war. We don't know who the enemy is.'

'I would not be looking past Marryat at this stage. Those big ranchers get too greedy. I know he claims to have been threatened but my guess is that he is only trying to divert suspicion.'

Hogan agreed that Marryat was the most likely suspect but excused himself when he saw Perez signalling to him. The half-breed was talking to Jack Connors, a hand from one of the neighbouring spreads. He said, when Hogan joined them: 'Jack here might be able to throw some light on some of the funny things that are happening here. Tell Ned, Jack, what you just told me.'

Connors was a weather-beaten cowhand who had worked all over the West and was regarded as one whose opinions could be respected.

'I have seen something like this before, Ned. I was caught up in a range war in New Mexico. As it happened, my side lost but the ones who won hired a range detective. He started leaving notes around and folks started getting shot.'

'I would imagine that a range detective would be a lawman,' Hogan said.

Connors gave a bitter smile. 'Some might have been once, but mostly they are just hired killers, paid by the big cattle barons. They justify their murders by claiming that their victims were rustlers and the law looks the other way. Some of them charge as much as five hundred dollars to kill a man.'

'The only one around here with that sort of money would be Marryat,' Perez said.

Hogan remembered the wrongly branded calves and realized that they presented the sort of evidence that a range detective needed to justify his murder. He asked: 'Do all these range detectives leave warning notes?'

'I can't say for sure, but Henry Power, the one who was in New Mexico, sure did. He left a warning and a couple of days later the poor devil concerned would be shot from long range if he had not already left the district.'

'What did this Power character look like?'

'I don't know and I don't think many others do either. He would arrive in a place, hole up on some big cattleman's spread, do his killing and disappear again.'

'I could be next on his list,' Hogan said.

Connors chuckled. 'The range detective might have to wait his turn. From what I hear you also have Ace Collins after your hide. He did not appreciate your last meeting with him. I reckon there could be at least two men gunning for you, Ned. You'll need to be mighty careful stepping out of your door in the mornings.'

Hogan excused himself and worked his way through the mourners to find Ellie. To his relief, Sam Hockley was nowhere to be seen. 'I'll have to be getting back to the ranch,' he said. 'I'll try to drop over to your place through the week.'

'That would be nice,' Ellie told him with a smile. 'We could go for a ride somewhere. I get sick of the house and would much rather be out on my pony.'

Reluctantly Hogan said: 'That might not be a good idea. There are a couple of people gunning for me and I don't want to put you in the way of flying lead. When we get this mess fixed, we'll do a lot more riding.'

'This is awful, Ned. When is it going to end?'

'Soon, I hope. I'll ride over through the week sometime.'

Next morning Hogan carefully studied the house's surroundings before leaving it. He went from window to window looking for possible sites where a rifleman could be hiding. There were some trees on a hill about 300 yards away, and a couple of sheds and the barn were potential danger spots. Then he saw Perez walking about and knew that he had already scouted the area. The half-breed had reasoned that nobody was after him and made sure that he had a good look around before his boss emerged.

They had a quick breakfast and planned their work for the day. Perez would go out to the cattle and see if he could discover any more wrongly branded calves. Hogan decided to visit some of the neighbours and see what information he could glean.

'What horse are you taking today?' Perez asked.

'I might give that sorrel mare a ride. She

30

needs some work.'

'Sure does. She's one of those rattle-brained things that will never stand still. I'm not sure you'll ever get her to settle down.'

'Neither am I, but while I'm riding her one of our better horses is resting.'

The rifleman sat patiently in the clump of young pines that concealed him while allowing a full view of the Rocking H front gate. He was not sure that Hogan would come out through that gate but was ready if he did. Manhunting required patience and the assassin was prepared to wait. He knew that Hogan had not been frightened by his note and was the natural leader for the ranchers along Warbonnet Creek. He had to die. He had set his sights at 200 yards so that they would be just right for anyone at the gate.

Movement caught his eye and a rider on a bright sorrel horse came around the corner of the ranch house. The horse was tossing its head and dancing about and would present a difficult target but there would not be so much movement as the rider came through the gate.

The man with the long Springfield rifle raised the weapon to his shoulder.

Hogan was at the gate but leaned down to undo the catch. In doing so he was partly obscured by the gatepost.

The unseen hunter eased back the big musket hammer on the rifle.

Hogan came through but turned the horse again and leaned down to fasten the catch. Again he presented an awkward angle. With the gate secure he turned the mare and was looking squarely at the rifleman's position. The front of his blue shirt showed clearly above the horse's ears.

With the foresight on the middle of the blue shirtfront, the waiting assassin squeezed the trigger.

FOUR

The sorrel mare tossed her head as the rifle discharged and the bullet meant for Hogan struck her squarely in the forehead. A brain-shot horse falls suddenly and the mare's legs collapsed before her rider fully comprehended what had happened.

Hogan's right leg was trapped beneath the fallen animal. He was aware that someone had shot at him but had no idea of the shooter's location. He drew his Colt and peered cautiously over the mare's carcass. As he did so another bullet buzzed past his head and buried itself in the gatepost nearby.

Perez came running from the corral, snatching the carbine from his saddle as he came. He was in time to see the puff of smoke from the second shot and threw a few rapid-fire slugs into the pines. All missed by a wide margin but they served notice that the lurking rifleman now had to contend with something more dangerous than an unsuspecting victim.

'There's plenty of time, Hogan,' the man said as he crept from his position and sought the horse he had concealed a short distance away.

Perez ran to the gate and crouched behind the gatepost. He dared not take his eyes off the pines on the hill. 'Are you all right, Ned?'

'I will be when I get out from under this horse. Did you see where that murdering coyote is?'

'I saw powder smoke in those pines on the hill but that's all. I don't know if he's still there. I can hear a horse coming up the road. Someone's keen to join the fun but I'm not sure which side he's on.'

Sam Hockley rounded a corner of the road, spurring his mount as he came. He saw the scene at the gate and galloped up to the others.

'Be careful, Sam. There's someone on the hill with a rifle,' Hogan called.

Hockley hauled his mount to a stop and came out of the saddle as though it was red-hot. As he hit the ground he dragged the carbine from its boot and placed his horse between himself and the hill. 'Did you see him?' he asked as he peered across his saddle.

'Didn't see a damn thing,' Hogan complained.

'Me neither,' Perez admitted.

'I'll try to shelter you with my horse,' Hockley offered. 'While your hand tries to get you out from under, I'll keep a close eye on that hill in case our friend is still there.'

It took a considerable effort but eventually Perez was able to move the dead mare just enough for Hogan to crawl clear. He struggled to his feet and undid the saddle cinch. The two of them managed to drag the saddle free and Hogan retrieved the carbine that had been trapped under the horse. He checked it over and apart from a few scratches on the butt, the weapon was in good order. 'At least my rifle is not smashed but that bastard still owes me for a horse,' he said grimly. As he levered a cartridge into the breech, he told the others: 'Keep your eyes on those trees. I'm going to see if anyone is still there.'

When Hogan eventually reached the trees, he found that his would-be killer had left the scene. An empty .45/70 shell betrayed the man's firing position and scuff-marks in the grass showed that he had been waiting for some time and had frequently changed positions. After looking around for a couple of minutes, he rejoined the others.

They discussed what had happened and reached the conclusion that a belated pursuit would be unlikely to succeed.

'If I had been a bit closer when the shooting started, I might have been more helpful,' Hockley said apologetically.

'And you might have been shot instead of me,' Hogan reminded him. 'That madman is after any small rancher and the description fits you as much as it does the rest of us. But I'm mighty glad you turned up when you did. It put an end to what looked like a very bad situation. Thanks for that.'

'Don't mention it. I was just having a look around the valley when I heard the shots. There's work waiting for me at the ranch, so I'd better get back.'

When Hockley left, Perez went to the horse pasture and brought back a pair of wagon-horses complete with collars and trace-chains. They hooked the team to the dead mare and dragged her well away from the road and the gate onto a large sheet of exposed rock. Then they collected dead wood and piled it on and around the carcass.

They were splashing coal-oil on the wood when a rider leading a pack-horse came down the road. As he got closer they saw that he was a middle-aged man, an itinerant cowhand by the look of him.

'Howdy,' the stranger said. 'Looks like you've

had a bit of bad luck there.'

'That's right. Someone shot one of my horses,' Hogan told him. 'Did you see anyone along the trail?'

'Not a soul. You're the first people I've seen since leaving Muddy Creek. I'm Wesley Charlton. I've been workin' up north but now I'm headin' back to Colorado. Was that horse shot accidental or on purpose?'

'Accidentally. The bullet was meant for me. I'm Ned Hogan and this is Juán Perez. Would you care to have a cup of coffee with us before we start this cremation?'

'Thanks, but I'll keep goin'. It looks like there's trouble out this way and I'm stayin' out of it. There's a job waitin' for me in Colorado if I don't take too long gettin' there.'

'You could probably pick up a bit of ranch work around here if you wanted it,' Perez suggested.

Charlton shook his head. 'There's too much trouble brewin' here. I heard about it in town and I know it ain't just gossip. I was in there a week ago and who should be walkin' out of the sheriff's office, but Henry Power. There's trouble wherever that mean sonofabitch goes. I don't want to get caught up in no range war.'

The name caught Hogan's attention but he tried to appear casual. 'I've heard about Power, but nobody knows what he looks like. Where did you see him before?'

'He was a lawman years ago and I saw him in a town in Kansas. Later I heard he became a bounty hunter and then a range detective.'

'What does he look like?' Hogan asked.

'He's around forty, pretty ordinary in looks with light-brown hair and a moustache. I reckon he'd be about average in height and build but he's the sort of *hombre* you'd pass in the street and hardly notice. He has a slight limp and always wears flat-heeled boots. The story is that someone wounded him once and one ankle ain't quite right. He carries one gun out of sight and was said to be an extra-good rifle shot but he didn't have no rifle when I saw him.'

'And you saw him in Muddy Creek?'

'Sure did. He was laughin' with that fancy-pants sheriff they got there, so I says to myself, Wesley, my boy, if he's comin' here, I'm leavin'. That mean sonofabitch wouldn't be payin' no social visits.'

They chatted for a few more minutes and then Charlton wished them luck and rode away. When he was out of sight Hogan said to Perez: 'Let's go back up that hill and have another look at that shooter's tracks.'

The ground was covered with knee-high

grass except for places where there were open areas of exposed rock. It was easy to see where their quarry had gone through the grass, but he had left no discernible footprints.

'I think we are wasting our time,' Hogan said. 'It's no trouble to see where he went but I don't think we will find any decent tracks.'

'Don't give up yet. Let's see where he left his horse. He wouldn't tie it on rock in case it made a noise or even slipped over and if the horse was there any length of time it would have trodden down the long grass. We might find a track there.'

It was easy to see where the horse had been and two piles of fresh manure showed that it had been standing there for a couple of hours. They saw hoof-marks but, at first, no clear boot-tracks.

Suddenly Perez chuckled. 'A great pair of trackers we are.' He pointed to a manure pile. 'Look there.'

A boot-print showed clearly in the soft, green mess. The boot had a large flat heel, unlike the smaller Cuban heels that most cowmen preferred for riding.

'A man ain't real fussy what he steps in when he needs to get on his horse in a hurry,' the half-breed said.

'I think that man now has a name,' Hogan

said. 'From what Charlton told us, we are looking at Henry Power's track. We know he's in
the area. The next job is to find out where he is
hiding.'

FIVE

Ace Collins reined in his horse and pointed to the column of black smoke rising against the cloudless blue sky to the south. 'Looks like a decent fire over there.'

Marryat urged his big, black horse onto the ridge. He always rode big horses in the belief that they made him look more imposing. 'That's coming from Hogan's Rocking H. I hope it's his house burning down.'

'So do I,' Collins said fervently. 'And I hope he's in it. It might be better for him if he is because I intend to square accounts with him soon. He caught me by surprise the other day but he won't do that again.'

'You will have to wait a while, Ace. There are a few other things that I need you for. When they are fixed up you can do what you like with Hogan if he's still around. Now, let's get home.'

As he turned his mount away, Collins looked back over his shoulder. The column of smoke had given him an idea.

Hogan and Perez had to stay around the fire in case the wind should carry sparks and cause spot fires in the vicinity. They were busily kicking unburnt ends of logs into the flames when Mike Casey and Ellie arrived.

'I hope you are not cooking dinner,' Ellie joked as she halted her grey pony. Then the smile disappeared. 'Sam Hockley told us someone tried to kill you this morning.'

'That's right, but that rattle-brained sorrel mare put her head in the way – about the only sensible thing she ever did.'

'You were lucky,' Casey said. 'Let's hope I have the same luck. I got a warning note this morning and so did Emil Bohm, further down the creek. It seems like our part of the world is getting mighty dangerous. Bohm reckons he's selling up. With a wife and three little kids, he can't afford to take risks.'

'What about you, Mike?'

It was Ellie who answered. 'We are staying. There are five of us and we can all handle guns. Nobody's driving us from our home.'

'I've been trying to talk Jean and Ellie into visiting Jean's sister in Nebraska until this mess is over but you know what they are like.'

Hogan shook his head. 'Women have always been a bit of a mystery to me, Mike. I'm hardly qualified to give opinions there, but I did learn something this morning. Did you happen to see a man named Charlton going down the road ? He was leading a pack-horse.'

'Sure did. What's he got to do with things?'

'He told us that he saw a range detective named Henry Power in Muddy Creek. He was with Nick Templeman.'

'Well I'll be damned.'

'You shouldn't say that, Pa,' Ellie corrected. 'You know that Mother doesn't like you cussing.'

'I'll cuss when the occasion demands it, young lady. Now, Ned, where was I – oh yes, Henry Power. How can you be sure that he's behind this trouble?'

'I'm not certain, but that possibility is worth considering. Charlton told us that he wears flat-heeled boots because of an old ankle injury. I found the print of that kind of boot up where the shooter was hidden this morning.'

'Lots of men wear flat-heeled boots. Not everyone rides a lot. Just on its own that's not much proof.'

'I know that but it's a start. I also have a rough idea of what Power looks like.'

'That might be helpful, We don't see a lot of strangers here. What does he look like?'

'He's medium height and build with light-brown hair and a moustache, around forty and has a slight limp. He carries a gun but keeps it out of sight, probably in a shoulder holster or something like that. Have you seen anyone like that around?'

Casey scratched his chin and thought for a while, 'Can't say I have. But if he's around here it's a wonder someone hasn't seen him.'

'Not necessarily. He seems to travel by night and holes up somewhere during the day.'

'Probably at Marryat's ranch,' Ellie suggested.

Hogan nodded in agreement. 'Marryat is the only one I know around here who can afford to pay what Power is supposed to charge.'

'There is also the possibility that the person behind this might not be from around here,' Ellie said. 'It could be some of our Muddy Creek businessmen. For example Nick Meyers handles all the legal work for miles around, knows everyone's business and he's not short of money.'

'Nick's very close-mouthed about his business but he has a very good reputation,' Casey said. 'It's highly unlikely that he would be involved in something like this. Now what do

44

we do about this Power character? Should we be telling our neighbours to watch for him?'

Hogan replied: 'Let's wait a while, and see what else we learn. Meanwhile, Mike, don't use the roads if you are moving around. This killer might be a stranger to the area and might not know his way about as well as we do. He is probably watching the road so stay off it. Go cross-country when you can and take the long way around. Don't go anywhere alone. And watch that he does not try to pick you off when you first walk out of your house in the morning.'

'We have very good dogs. They let us know if anyone is about,' said Ellie.

'That may be but if this person is the experienced killer we think he is, he would have found ways of getting around dogs. Be very careful.'

When the Caseys had left Perez turned to Hogan. 'It seems to me that we have forgotten the one man who could tell us about this Power *hombre*. We should be asking Templeman some questions.'

'We would only be wasting our time, Juán. He would never admit to being involved and he would be too scared to say anything in case Power came after him. We might get around to Templeman later but right now, I reckon we'll get out on the range and see if we see anything unusual. We might also drift over Marryat's way and see if we can watch a few comings and goings there.'

'You don't seem worried about being shot.'

'I am, but the odds are on our side at present. This shooter does most of his travel by night and picks single targets. There will be two of us and we know the country well. There's not much chance that Power or whoever it is can be lying in wait when he doesn't know where we will be.'

'He knows that you will be here every night, Ned. He's sure to have another try at you.'

'I know that, but the more we can learn about him the less chance he has of succeeding.'

'You also have the little matter of Ace Collins. Don't forget him.'

SIX

Collins saw the rider coming through the boundary gate. It was part of his job to check any strangers before Marryat showed himself.

The horseman was young, with long, untidy fair hair. He looked about him as he rode as though expecting trouble. His dress was that of a working cowhand but the nickel-plated Colt with the elaborately carved ivory grips contradicted that assumption. He wore it butt-forward on his left hip in an expensive leather holster. Matt Pritchard lived by his gun and gave it the best of attention.

Collins walked to the edge of the veranda. 'Howdy, Matt,' he greeted. 'You took your time getting here. Step down and come and meet the boss.'

'What happened to your face, Ace? It looks like you struck some trouble.'

'Nothing that won't be fixed soon. What took you so long?'

Pritchard gave a wry smile. 'I couldn't come by the shortest route. There were a couple of counties I had to go around on account of some narrow-minded sheriffs who were rather keen to meet me.'

'That won't happen around here. Marryat has the sheriff jumping through hoops.'

'What's happening here? The telegram didn't tell me much.'

'There's a range war shaping up and a couple of small ranchers who seem determined to cause trouble. You and I are to look after the boss's interests and make sure nobody steals his cows or fills him with lead. If some of the other side should get shot in the process, the law won't be trying too hard to lay murder charges. Come inside now and meet Mr Marryat. You'll be seeing a lot of him in the next few weeks.'

Sam Hockley brought the news about Marryat's new gunslinger. He arrived at Hogan's door just as the evening meal was finished.

'I heard a bit of important news today, Ned. My cowhand met a rider he knows who works for Marryat. It seems that he's hired another

48

gunman, a bad character from Texas named Pritchard.'

'Come in, Sam, and have a seat. Would you care for a cup of coffee?'

'No thanks, Ned. I won't stay long.'

Hogan smiled slightly. 'There must be something about my coffee. Juán here is the only one besides me who will drink it and I suspect he only does it because he gets paid to do it.'

'Think yourself lucky that I do. I know a lot of *hombres* who would not drink your coffee if you paid them,' Perez retorted.

'I can't say I've heard of this Pritchard, Sam, but for all the news we get, we are lucky to know what's happening here without hearing who's shooting who in Texas.'

'What worries me is that Marryat seems to be gathering a few gunmen. He could be planning an all-out range war. I wonder if we should start getting our men together. Do you think we should hold a meeting and start making plans to defend ourselves?'

'I'm not sure. If we look to be getting ready for a war it might only panic the other side into doing something desperate.'

Hockley looked surprised. 'You don't think what's been happening is already desperate?'

'I do but we need to know who we are fighting before we figure out how to fight them.'

'It has to be Marryat and his gunmen. Who else could it be?'

'I don't know yet, Sam but this lone gunman seems a different breed from Collins. He's seems to be a lot smarter.'

'That would not be hard,' Perez observed from his seat near the kitchen stove.

Nothing had been resolved by the time Hockley had to leave. He said that he would confer with some of the other ranchers, seek their opinions and try to work out a plan that suited the majority.

'Be careful on the road tonight,' Hogan warned as the rancher mounted his horse.

'Our killer is a long-range rifleman, Ned. He won't have much luck late at night when it's dark.'

'He might change his style. Go cross-country and you'll be a lot safer.'

Hogan and Perez turned in. They wanted to be out on the range in the morning as soon as it was light. While pretending to look at the Rocking H cattle, they would really be searching for anything unusual.

After breakfast next morning they saddled their horses and rode to the back of the ranch, where they opened some rails and rode into the unfenced country beyond.

The year had been a good one and the cattle

they saw were fat and healthy. A few older longhorns took off as soon as they sighted the riders but the crosses of more recently introduced Durham and Hereford strains merely glanced up from their feeding as the horsemen passed them. As cattlemen both had seen enough bad years to appreciate the good ones. They were enjoying the ride until Hogan happened to glance behind him.

A column of thick, black smoke was rising in the sky. It appeared to be coming from his ranch.

SEVEN

They were too late to do anything to save the house. The roof had collapsed by the time the pair had spurred their lathered horses to the scene of the fire.

Mike Casey and his second son, Dave, were already there but had arrived too late.

As he surveyed the ruins Perez remarked: 'This man who owes you a horse now also owes you a house, Ned.'

'Speaking of horses,' Dave Casey said, 'your horses have all been let out of their pasture. Dad and I saw them as we came up the road. They're scattered to hell and gone.'

'They won't go far with all this good grass about. I'll round them up later.'

'We thought you might have been in that fire, Ned. Ellie wanted to come but I thought it wiser if she didn't. She'll be relieved to know that you didn't come to any harm,' Mike Casey said.

Hogan seemed lost for words. He looked at the ruins and knew that his enemies had scored a telling blow against him. The building itself could be replaced but personal papers and mementos of his earlier life were gone. So many small items essential for daily life had also been destroyed.

Perez had lost all but the clothing he wore, but cowhands travel light and his loss was nothing like Hogan's.

Hockley arrived with his hired hand. They had ridden hard. He dismounted and introduced Wilton Norris, a large, powerfully built man in his thirties. The lower half of his face was covered by a short, black beard that only added to the man's generally tough appearance. He said little, just enough to be sociable, but his restlessly moving eyes indicated that he was taking in all that occurred around him.

'Sorry we couldn't get here sooner, Ned. Wilt saw the smoke first and thought it was a house burning but by the time we saddled up it was probably too late. If there is anything I can do to help, just name it.'

'Thanks, Sam. I might think of something later but right now I'm having trouble gettting my ideas sorted out. They didn't set fire to the barn so Juán and I can live there temporarily.'

'You can have your meals with us,' Mike Casey volunteered.

Perez walked over to his horse. 'While you are deciding what to do I'll have a look for tracks and round up our horses.'

'I'll come with you,' Dave Casey said.

'Did you leave Tom at home guarding Jean and Ellie?' Hogan asked Casey as they stood by the smoking ruins.

'Yes. We don't know where this killer will strike next.'

Hockley moved out of the way of drifting smoke and said: 'You took a risk, Mike. Don't forget that your name is on a death-list somewhere. What if this fire had been bait to lure you or Ned into a gunman's rifle sights?'

'I wasn't thinking like that at the time,' Casey admitted. 'I'm too used to riding about without having to worry. But you are right, Sam. I was a bit careless.'

'We'll all need to start thinking a bit more about what we do,' Hockley said. 'The two of you have received threats and so has Bohm. Because I am the new boy around here the killer seems to have forgotten me, but he'll realize that I'm here soon.'

They were still discussing a plan of action when Perez and Dave Casey came back

54

driving the horses ahead of them. They were well-bred animals and Hogan felt a sense of pride as they galloped past. The gates were open, so it was easy to herd the remuda back into the horse pasture.

'I don't know why whoever it was bothered to let the horses out,' Hockley said. 'Do you think someone intended to steal them and was frightened off?'

Mike Casey answered: 'Maybe it was to stop Ned getting a fresh horse and going after him. What do you reckon, Ned?'

'That could be, but with loose horses all over the place a lot of tracks would be blotted out, so that might have had something to do with it. I'll have to go to town this afternoon to make arrangements with the bank and order a few supplies, and also report this fire to Templeman, for all the good that will do.'

'Be careful on the road,' Hockley warned.

'I won't be on the road all that much. I can take a lot of routes where I don't have to travel by road. That's the big advantage of open range. I think I know this country better than that other murdering sonofabitch.'

'You and Juán should stay with us tonight,' Casey said. 'We have plenty of room in our bunkhouse and you can have your meals with us.'

55

'That's mighty good of you, Mike. We'll take you up on that offer. Juán can go with you now and I'll come straight there from town. I might be late coming in so don't wait up for me. I'll go straight to the bunkhouse and see you in the morning. I'll get a better travelling-horse and be on my way.'

He selected Diamond, a black-footed bay horse with a white diamond on its forehead. The gelding was tough with a smooth stride at all paces.

As Hogan was cinching his saddle in place Hockley said: 'That's a nice horse. You won't be long getting to town on him.'

'It will still take me two hours. Unless there's a very good reason, I don't push my horses hard when I am travelling. I like to keep them fit enough to use the next day if I have to.'

Hogan took his leave of the others and rode out through the rails at the back of the ranch. He turned his mount to the north-west. Diamond was fresh and wanted to increase his pace but the rider checked him lightly. Where the ground was soft and fairly level he allowed the horse to canter but where it was rough or steep Diamond dropped back to his fast amble.

The presence of a killer made Hogan more

sensitive to his surroundings. There were clusters of rocks, clumps of trees, flood-scoured gullies and ridges that could all shelter a waiting rifleman. He told himself that it would only be sheer coincidence if the killer was in such an isolated area, but he was still anxious. He knew he was close to the end of his ride when he came to a farmer's wire fence. Turning along it, he followed the wire down to the road and saw the buildings of Muddy Creek in the distance.

The muddy creek that gave the town its name was at the foot of a slight hill and he allowed Diamond to have a drink before continuing the ride The town was comparatively new but already looked old. The hastily built buildings had not weathered well. Originally it had been built by speculators anticipating a railroad branch line that never came. Now it supplied local ranchers and farmers with supplies and services that were only available in towns. There was only one street with private houses at each end and some commercial buildings in the middle.

The Longhorn saloon was one of the biggest buildings but only two horses were hitched to the rail in front of it. Few ranch men visited town in the middle of a working day. As he rode past Hogan noticed that both animals bore Marryat's brand. To avoid any confrontations he decided to keep out of the saloon.

Hogan's first stop was the bank. He had to find out how much money he had. Arthur Welch, the manager, was said to be so tight that he squeaked when he walked and hated parting with money even when it was not his. He carefully scrutinized the bank records and noted that the rancher had enough funds to justify a new check-book. As though doing Hogan a great favour he passed over the book but warned him that he was not to overdraw the account. Though he did not say as much, he had heard of impending trouble along Warbonnet Creek and did not relish the idea of someone dying while they owed the bank money.

Armed with the checkbook Hogan went to Murphy's general store. He knew Perez's size from writing mail orders on his behalf so he ordered some new clothing for both of them. Blankets, cooking utensils, food and delivery charges gave his bank account a battering but he needed them. As an afterthought he bought some more rifle and revolver cartridges. The goods would be delivered in two days' time but in the meantime Perez and he could stay at Casey's.

Having attended to the more pressing issues, he had one last task: a visit to Sheriff Templeman.

EIGHT

Templeman was reading a newspaper when Hogan entered the office. At first he pretended not to notice him.

'I'm looking for a lawman,' the rancher said sarcastically. 'Would you know where I might find one?'

The sheriff pretended surprise. 'Oh, it's you, Hogan. Come to turn yourself in for rustling, have you?'

'No, I've come to tell you that somebody burned my house down this morning.'

Templeman put his newspaper aside. 'Do you know who did it?'

'No, but I mean to find out.'

'Did anyone see a person setting fire to your house?'

'No.'

'Let me tell you something, my friend. A lot of houses burn down because they burn a lot of

60

pine and soot builds up in the chimneys. It catches fire, spreads to the dry shingle roof and the whole place goes up in flames. There's nothing unusual about that.'

'It so happens that I check the stove if I'll be away for the day and make sure that the fire dies out. Also this "accidental" fire somehow let the horses out of my horse pasture.'

'Someone was probably careless with the gate or some cunning old pony figured out how to undo it. We have both seen that happen.'

Hogan could see that the sheriff was determined to downplay all that had occurred. He had one more try. 'Somebody tried to shoot me the other day. He missed and killed my horse. I think it was the same person who shot Walter Hill. People along Warbonnet Creek are getting death-threats. Casey and Bohm have got them as well as me.'

The sheriff sat back in his chair. 'Marryat told me that he got one too. He reckons that you sent it. Do you have any idea of who else could be sending these threats?'

'Yes, I do.'

Templeman's eyes narrowed. He had not been expecting a positive reply. 'Who?'

'A friend of yours, Henry Power.'

The sheriff looked shocked but quickly recovered his composure. 'Never heard of him.

Who is he? What makes you think he's a friend of mine?'

'I'll answer your last question first. He was seen here with you about two weeks ago. He is also a range detective, hiring out his gun to some of the big cattlemen's associations. He murders people on the excuse that they are rustlers, and the law looks the other way.'

Templeman was suddenly out of his depth and commenced to bluster. 'That's total rubbish. I don't know this Power and would not allow such operations where I am responsible for the law. I don't associate with murderers. If you dare say that in public, Hogan, I'll sue you.'

The rancher looked about. There were no witnesses. 'Now I'm going to tell you something in private. You are as crooked as a dog's hind-leg. You are also a liar and I will do all in my power to get you into jail along with your murdering friend.'

'I'm the sheriff here. You can't say that to me.'

'I just did and I know that you don't have the guts to do anything about it. You could prove me wrong on that last point any way you like but you won't try – at least not when I am facing you.'

With his hand hovering over his gun butt,

Hogan backed out of the office.

He was hungry so went to the small eatery near the end of the street for a quick meal before starting the ride home. He was paying Judy, the waitress when she looked beyond him through the window. She made no secret of her dislike for the sheriff. 'That's funny, Templeman must have changed his mind. I saw him a minute ago heading for the saloon, He looked like he needed a drink. But he wasn't there long enough for a drink and I just saw him riding out of town. He looked like he was in a hurry. It's not often we see our sheriff doing anything energetic.'

Hogan was about to make some flippant remark when a thought occurred to him. He remembered the two horses wearing Marryat's brand that were hitched outside the saloon. Ordinary cowhands were not allowed to go to town on working days and neither horse was the big mount that Marryat habitually rode. He already knew the answer when he asked: 'Judy, have you seen Ace Collins today?'

'Sure did. Him and another jasper that looked like a gunfighter rode in about two hours ago. They've been in the saloon ever since.' She glanced through the window again. 'Well, speak of the devil. They've just come out again. They're going toward the bank, probably going to rob it while the sheriff is gone.'

'I'll have to go out through your kitchen, Judy. See you next time I'm in town.'

He left the eatery by way of a side alley. He peered around the corner of the building. He saw Collins and another man emerge from the bank. They were heading for the general store. While they were inside he crossed the street and unhitched his horse. He was in the saddle by the time the pair emerged from the store. They saw him and ran toward him, drawing their guns as they came.

He wheeled Diamond and was none too gentle with the spurs. The bay horse jumped into his stride. Glancing over his shoulder the rancher saw the two gunmen running for their horses.

Collins tried a long-range shot at the rapidly moving target but his companion was not inclined to waste lead. Both men quickly mounted and turned their horses in pursuit.

On the other side of the town, Templeman heard the shot that Collins had fired. One shot, that was good, he told himself. His most dangerous enemy had just been removed. Whistling a tune, he turned his horse and rode back to Muddy Creek.

Hogan had gained 200 yards before the chase started. Diamond's sire was a Kentucky thoroughbred and now his owner's life depended upon his choice of breeding. By contrast Marryat had never bothered much about the breeding of his cowponies. He had plenty of them and if one failed it was easy to get a replacement. His horses were rough and plain-looking but they had been raised under hard conditions, where only the strongest survived. They were in working condition and could be expected to give a good account of themselves. Driven on by raking spurs they tried to close the gap between hunters and hunted.

The riders cleared the town and raced past the small farms on the settlement's edge. People working outside watched curiously for as long as the horsemen were in sight.

As soon as he could, Hogan turned off the road and headed for the open range, where he hoped that his knowledge of the country might be an advantage. He steadied his mount. The race would be a long one and he could only survive by keeping Diamond fit to run. A gunfight with two professional gunmen was out of the question.

'We're gaining on him,' Pritchard said. 'Our horses might just outlast that one he's riding and he's running away from witnesses. I think we'll get him, Ace, and there will be nobody about to see what happens.'

'He's mine,' Collins shouted and applied the spurs again so that his horse shot two lengths clear of Pritchard's. Already he was imagining the satisfaction of squaring accounts with the man who had humiliated him so badly.

Hogan glanced over his shoulder and saw that Collins had narrowed the gap between them. Diamond was still running strongly but as he swept up a ridge an idea came to him. If all went well he would be able to use his local knowledge to turn the tables.

NINE

Hogan knew the area well and usually avoided it. There was a prairie-dog village at the foot of the ridge but it was masked by low bushes. When his mount topped the hill he was hidden from the others so he set a course that would avoid the hazard he knew was ahead. Then he turned back on his original path so that it looked as though he had ridden straight down the hill. He lost a bit of his lead and was just on his previous track when the two riders came over the crest. They yelled in triumph when they saw how much they had gained on their quarry. Recklessly they gave their horses rein as they plunged stiff-legged down the slope.

When they hit the level ground the gunmen drove in their spurs. Too late they saw the holes and bare earth around them. The black horse that Collins rode stumbled in a hole but somehow managed to stay on its feet.

Pritchard's buckskin was not so lucky. It crashed down in a shower of red dust, throwing the rider out ahead of it. The animal rose before its rider but its broken hindleg was swinging loosely.

Collins might not have seen what happened to his companion because he was concentrating on Hogan. The latter's horse had extended its lead slightly but the gunman still had hopes of running him down.

Seeing that he only had Collins to contend with, Hogan decided that he was through running. He drew his Winchester, set his mount into a sliding stop and jumped from the saddle. He levered a cartridge into the breech and threw the rifle to his shoulder.

The move took Collins by surprise. Frantically he hauled on the reins but his mount was already too close to Hogan. A fifty-yard shot with a revolver from a moving horse was most unlikely to hit its target but a man on foot with a rifle had a comparatively easy task at the same range. Even as the gunman drew his Colt and fired a despairing shot, he knew that his luck had run out. Hogan fired just as Collins was trying to turn his horse away. The bullet took him in the side and spilled him from the saddle. He hit the ground, rolled against the trunk of a pine sapling and lay still.

A bullet kicked up dust beside him and the rancher saw that Pritchard was trying some very long-range shooting with his Winchester. Feeling that he had used up his supply of luck for the day, he remounted his horse and, ignoring the shots, caught the reins of the dead man's horse which had moved closer to his for comfort. Then Hogan cantered away leaving Pritchard cursing, miles from anywhere and on foot.

When he was far enough away from the gunman, Hogan knotted the black horse's reins and looped them behind the saddle horn. Left to its own devices and with the reins preventing it from grazing, the horse would head straight for its home range.

He had few regrets about shooting Collins. He suspected that Ace and his companion had been in Muddy Creek celebrating the burning of his ranch house.

Marryat was fuming. His two high-priced bodyguards had been missing all day. He stormed about the ranch and in his anger was giving vague and contradictory orders to his men. The working cowhands had little regard for the two gunmen and were secretly pleased that they were out of the way.

The little rancher, after hours of impatient waiting, finally retired to his office to catch up on some correspondence. 'Tell me as soon as that pair come back,' he ordered his cook.

He had no sooner started to sort out his papers than the cook called to him. 'Mr Marryat, there's a loose horse just trotted up to the front gate.'

'Tell one of the men to go down and get it. I can't be worried every time some useless cowboy falls off his horse.'

He resumed his work and about ten minutes later heard high-heeled boots and dragging spurs on the veranda floor. Gus Scott, his foreman, came to the office door.

Marryat looked up from his work and said angrily: 'Well?'

'That loose horse, boss – it's the one that Ace Collins rode today.'

'So he let it get away from him somehow. The walk home will do him good. Any sign of Pritchard?'

Scott shook his head. 'Ace's horse was deliberately turned loose. The reins were looped back around the saddle horn. There's no sign of Pritchard either. Something's gone wrong.'

Marryat threw down his pen and swore. He shouted at Scott: 'Get the men out and backtrack that horse. Use your initiative, Gus.' Then he had second thoughts. Without his gunmen he felt very insecure. 'Leave a couple of men here,' he ordered.

Soon after sundown the rifleman mounted his horse and headed for the open range. He had studied a rough map of the area and calculated where he thought Hogan would travel on his return journey. The rancher would have to cross the long range of hills that formed the northern edge of the Warbonnet valley. The patches of brush, the scattered areas of pines and outcrops of rock provided him with plenty of concealment but they might also protect his target. He would need to be reasonably close to be sure of his victim. He was not worried about killing an innocent traveller because he knew that anyone abroad at night would most likely be a Warbonnet Creek man. Any shooting at all would add to the fear of the small ranchers but Hogan was his main target. He seemed to be the unofficial leader of the community.

There was a moon but patches of cloud were drifting across it and at times restricted visibility. The killer was a patient man and knew that there would be other opportunities if his hunt failed that night. He concealed his horse carefully in a patch of trees on the other side of the ridge. If Hogan's horse should catch the scent of another animal it might betray his presence and the rifleman left nothing to luck. He believed that a man who planned properly made his own luck.

The moonlight clearly showed a track that the cattle had made over the ridge going to and from water. Cows always worked out the easiest grades in steep country and experienced cattlemen knew that it was easier to travel on cow tracks. He was gambling that Hogan was no exception.

Selecting what he thought to be the most likely ambush site, the killer settled down to wait. Time seemed to drag and he found himself frequently checking the large watch that he carried in his vest pocket.

Smoking was out of the question but he fished a block of chewing-tobacco from his pocket, cut off a piece with his pocket-knife and started to chew. It gave him something to do while he waited.

A sound carried through the night silence, faint at first but then becoming louder. The waiting man peered into the gloom, straining his eyes to catch a glimpse of the approaching rider. Gradually an indistinct blur changed to a more definite, dark shape. Just as he raised his rifle a bank of clouds drifted across the moon and the rider was lost in shadow. He was on a cow track that would take him within a hundred yards of the shooter's position.

The clouds moved and the moonlight revealed the scene again. Hogan was no longer on the track he had been following. Instead of riding out of the hollow he was riding along it and moving away from the ambush. The watching man could see no reason for his target's change of direction. He did not appear to be alarmed.

The waiting killer was unaware that Hogan had left the track because he knew that it came out at a point along the creek that was too far from Casey's. He knew that half a mile away, at the end of the hollow, there was another path that would take him closer to his destination.

The rifleman had to act quickly. His target's horse was walking well and the range would soon increase. He squinted along his sights but had trouble distinguishing the foresight against the dark mass of the rider's body.

Gently he took up the slack on the trigger.

TEN

A bank of cloud covered the moon again and the rifleman cursed silently in frustration. He was tempted to fire but decided against it. An accurate shot could not be guaranteed. He could not afford to miss or have his victim escape wounded. There would be other opportunities.

Hogan would never know that for the second time that day he had experienced a brush with death. Eventually he reached Casey's and came through a gate on the back boundary. A faint glimmer of light in the distance told him that someone was waiting up for him. The dogs picked up his scent and barked furiously as he approached the house.

A door opened slightly and the rancher saw a figure peering out. The lamplight from inside glinted on what appeared to be a rifle barrel. 'Is that you, Ned?'

'It's me, Mike.'

'How did things go in town?'

'It's a long story. Just wait till I put my horse away and I'll tell you.'

'Put him in that small square corral. There's feed and water there for him. Then come up to the house. Jean's saved some dinner for you.'

When he made his way to the ranch house, Hogan found that Ellie had waited up for him too. Much of his weariness went when he saw her smiling face. 'It's been a big day,' he told them.

'We are sorry to hear about the house,' Ellie said. 'You and Juán can stay here as long as you like.'

'Were you able to get what you wanted in town?' Casey asked.

'Mostly,' he said with a wry smile. 'I arranged things as well as I could and even had time to win the lifelong hatred of Templeman. But leaving town was a bit hasty. Ace Collins and another gunman were there, probably celebrating the successful burning down of my house. I'm sure that Templeman told them I was in town and they came gunning for me. Meanwhile our sheriff rode out of town so that he would not be involved.'

Casey was about to swear but saw the glance his wife shot at him. 'That crooked—'

Again Jean glared at him and he fell silent.

'How did you get away?' Ellie prompted.

'They chased me out to the open range. Ace's friend rode his horse into a prairie-dog town and it came over. Ace thought I was going to keep running but as soon as I got him far enough from his friend, I turned around and picked him off with a rifle before he could really get in six-shooter range. I don't know if I killed him but I think I did. He was mighty keen on killing me.'

Casey looked worried. 'That's real bad. It's good that Collins is gone but it has given Marryat and Templeman the chance to start throwing their weight around. I think they'll call the shooting murder and come after you.'

'But it was self-defence.'

'Who saw it?'

'Only the other gunman. There were a few people working farms on the edge of town, though. They would be able to testify that they saw the other two chasing me.'

'Testimony won't matter, Ned.' Casey's voice was harsh with anger. 'You'll be shot trying to evade capture or attempting to escape. Nobody wants you talking in an open courtroom.'

A look of horror spread over Ellie's face. She had never envisaged a situation like the one that was suddenly unfolding. Feeling that she spoke for her family, she said: 'They'll have to fight us Caseys before they get you, Ned.'

Her father agreed. 'That's right. We can't let Marryat and his friends pick us off one at a time. Let's drag this out into the open. I know that a lot of the other small ranchers around here will stand with us.'

'Thanks for the offer, everyone, but it's best if you keep within the law. Someone should talk to Nick Meyers in town and see if he can give any legal advice that might help.'

'I'm not sure we can trust Meyers,' Casey said. 'He's the only one around here who knows everyone's business. Marryat would be his best customer and he's hardly likely to bite the hand that feeds him. Sam Hockley was only saying today that there are more lawyers working around the law than there are working within it.'

'You could be right, but don't worry too much about me. There is still a killer roaming about. I'm pretty sure it is Henry Power. When I mentioned that name to Templeman he got the shock of his life. He denied knowing him of course, but our sheriff is downright negligent with the truth. Templeman holds the key to all of this but he's unlikely to change sides.'

'Are you going to leave Warbonnet Creek, Ned?' Ellie's voice was quiet and she sounded fearful of the expected answer.

'Not unless I have to, Ellie, but I intend to make myself hard to find. There are plenty of places around here where I can hide. I'll keep in touch.'

Casey asked: 'How will we contact you?'

'If it's OK for Juán to stay here with you, I'll make sure that he knows where to find me. It's best if you don't know. That way you don't have to lie to protect me. I might need a bit of food from time to time and maybe some horse-feed but I'll be mighty hard to find. There's another thing, too. I can prowl around at night and might happen to find our mystery shooter. He won't know where to look for me now. But he can find you, Mike, and you are on his list. Get Juán to scout around for tracks every morning. When I leave here I'll go over to the bunkhouse and tell Juán what is happening.'

'I'll start getting some food together for you,' Jean Casey said. She turned to her husband. 'Get some horse feed from the barn, Mike.'

'Thanks a lot, folks, but just make it for a couple of days. I have to carry it all on one horse.'

Casey went into his bedroom and returned with a leather case that contained a pair of field glasses. 'Take these with you, Ned, and give them plenty of work. You have to see the people who are after you before they see you.'

Hogan protested. 'You might need them yourself, Mike.'

'No, I have a much stronger naval telescope that belonged to Jean's father. He was a seafaring man.'

'Use that telescope every morning, Mike, and have a good look around before anyone goes outside. You are in more danger than I am.'

'I have a few more guns behind me,' Casey reminded.

Hogan went to the bunkhouse, awoke Perez quietly and told him what had occurred. The half-breed left his bunk and came outside so that the two Casey brothers would not hear what was being planned. The fewer people who knew what was agreed upon, the safer it would be for all concerned.

He went to the corral and saddled Diamond. Casey came out of the barn with a small sack of feed and Ellie came from the house with a supply of food for Hogan. His saddle-bags were bulging by the time the supplies were stored away. The bags were in place and he was securing the feed-sack behind the cantle of his saddle when Casey wished him luck and left.

Ellie stood closer and sadness showed in her eyes. Then she smiled shyly and planted a kiss on his cheek. 'You look after yourself, Ned.'

He put out an arm to encircle her waist but she was already moving away. 'I'll be careful, Ellie, and I will be back. Thank you.'

For a brief instant the happenings along Warbonnet Creek were far from his mind. Then they came back with a rush and Hogan felt a surge of anger against those whose greed was causing so much misery.

With a heavy heart he mounted Diamond and rode out of the corral. No lights showed in the windows but in case Ellie was watching from hers, he waved before riding into the darkness. He wondered if he would ever see his favourite person again.

ELEVEN

As predicted, Sheriff Templeman rode up to Casey's ranch with a posse two days later. Three of the party were townsmen and Marryat had sent along two of his cowhands to protect his interests.

Casey came out of his front door as the horseman halted before the house. 'Are you looking for me?'

'Not at present,' Templeman sneered. 'No doubt I'll get around to you later but at present I'm looking for your friend Hogan.'

'You have the wrong ranch, Sheriff. He's not here. Did you try the Rocking H?'

'When did you see him last?'

'He came here the night before last but didn't say he was going anywhere special.'

Templeman leaned down on his saddle horn. 'What did he say?'

'What's this all about, Sheriff?'

'It's about murder, Casey. Hogan ambushed and killed Ace Collins. Did he forget to tell you that?'

The rancher glared at the sheriff, his anger rising. 'He told me that you set two gunmen onto him and then snuck out of town so that you would not be involved. He left Muddy Creek with two gunmen after him. I'm sure there would be a few witnesses to that fact. Ace Collins bit off more than he could chew and actually fired at Hogan before he got shot. If you checked his gun you would find that one chamber had been fired.'

A couple of possemen started to look doubtfully at each other. This version of events was totally different from what they had been told. For the first time they began to suspect that Templeman himself was involved.

'Lies – all lies,' the sheriff blustered. 'Hogan chose a time when I was out of town to start making trouble.'

'That ain't the way he told it and there were other people in town who saw what was going on. When this gets to court you're going to have a lot of awkward questions to answer. I hope the people who pull your strings have given you all the right answers.'

Templeman was livid. 'If you were twenty

years younger, Casey, I'd soon shut your lying mouth.'

'Don't let a few years stop you, Templeman. I can handle you any day of the week.'

Tom Casey emerged from the house and stood beside his father. 'I'm twenty years younger, Templeman, and I say the same thing. What are you going to do about it?'

One look at the brawny young rancher told the sheriff that his bluff had been called. 'I'll attend to you later. I won't forget this. Right now I have a murderer to catch.' With that threat, he wheeled the big palomino about and led his men from the ranch.

From a high ridge, Hogan had watched the scene through the field glasses, but had no idea of what had been said. Keeping out of sight he followed the posse and saw them go to his ranch and search the barn. After looking around for a while they went to Hill's ranch. He lost sight of them for a while because of the contours of the land. Half an hour later they reappeared, going back over their tracks, obviously aiming to enquire at Hockley's and Bohm's ranches. He knew they would find nothing there.

The light had all but gone before he glimpsed the posse again. They had moved out of the valley and into the unfenced range.

From there they set a course that would lead them straight to Marryat's. He guessed that Templeman would use the ranch as a base while he combed the countryside.

Marryat had mixed feelings when he saw the posse ride up. On one hand they added to his security, but he begrudged them the rations and horse feed that they might consume. Although he had to stay friendly with him, the rancher disliked Templeman. In his mind the sheriff was weak and unreliable.

Meanwhile Perez had set out on his first mission to resupply his employer. He knew that he would have to go to a place where Hogan had shot a cattle-killing bear. It was well-hidden in a big stand of pines. He spied a pair of empty saddle-bags and found a note in one. It instructed him to make his next drop in three days' time at a place where Hogan had once been thrown from a certain sorrel horse. If anyone should find the notes they would learn nothing from them. Leaving the full bags concealed, he put the empty ones on his saddle and, after looking around carefully, rode back to Casey's.

Marryat was in his usual bad mood as he questioned the sheriff about his progress to date. He was disappointed with the size of the posse and the fact that they did not have a really competent tracker among them. He knew that Hogan would not be easy to trap in territory where he had lived for years. As he and the sheriff ate that night in the ranch's special dining-room, he began asking questions. Templeman's answers gave him no reason for optimism.

'Nobody's talking,' the sheriff said. 'We rode around all day but didn't see a damn thing. I did find out something, though. Hogan's man Perez is still at Casey's. That new fellow, Hockley, accidentally let it slip. I reckon we should watch him and he might lead us to his boss.'

'He might be prepared to sell him out,' Marryat suggested. 'You can never trust a 'breed.'

'I'm not sure about this one. It might be a bit too soon to show our hand. Can you loan me a couple of men to keep watch on him? They are out here right on the scene and they know the country.'

'Will you pay their expenses if you use my men?'

'The posse rate is a dollar per day which is pretty close to cowhand's wages. I'm prepared to pay it.'

'What about horses?' Marryat demanded. 'You'll have to hire them too. I want fifty cents a day for them.'

'That's a bit steep, isn't it?'

The rancher's jaw set in a hard line. 'You can always go elsewhere and get your own men and horses.'

Templeman had to admit defeat. 'I suppose the town's funds can stand it. After all, we are looking at a murder here.'

'So what's the plan?'

'I head back to town and you set two men to watch Casey's ranch. They have to keep out of sight and follow that 'breed wherever he goes. Eventually he'll lead us to Hogan. Send a rider to town as soon as you hear anything positive.'

'Posse rates?' Marryat asked hopefully.

Templeman admitted defeat. 'Why not? Another dollar or two won't make a hell of a difference now.'

A few miles away Hogan was riding about under cover of darkness, moving slowly and looking for signs of anything unusual. The unknown killer worried him more than the sheriff because he knew that Mike Casey was on his death list.

Occasionally on his lonely rides he saw the distant lamplight shining through the windows at Casey's and was tempted to visit them, but he refrained from doing so. He did not want to put them in any more danger than they were in already.

He thought it best that he should patrol the vicinity of his friends' ranch looking for any intruders. Perez would scout the immediate area every morning. Casey had also taken to letting a couple of his dogs loose at night. These were old animals that never wandered far from home and they added greatly to the security around the buildings.

Henry Power, for he was the range detective, was beginning to feel frustrated. His nightly scouting forays were being detected by the dogs and, with Hogan gone, he had to get rid of Casey quickly before the fright wore off the other ranchers. Perez was a worry too. He would check the wind currents to see where scents would not carry to the dogs. And he would check for boot-prints or horse-tracks. It was becoming increasingly hard to get within rifle range of the house. The dogs had to go. Many ranches had strychnine on hand for wolf baits. He was sure that he would have no trouble obtaining a supply. Poisoning the dogs would alert Casey but at the same time it would open a wide gap in his defences. Briefly he considered shooting Perez, but the half-breed was not a major player and he would not be paid for the shooting.

Someone would have to die soon or his employer would not be pleased. The question was, who?

Hogan had found himself a vantage point where he had the best view of the surrounding countryside. He could see his own barn and the buildings at Casey's but there were stands of pines, patches of brush and uneven ground in between so he could not see the entire landscape.

Marryat had not been swamped with volunteers when he sought two riders to search for Hogan, but a couple of the less-principled volunteered. It was easier than range work.

Jock Cowdrey and Charley Winston rode out for their first day as posse members but really did not expect to see anything of Hogan. Indeed they hoped that they would not, because the man who shot Ace Collins could not be taken lightly.

Juán Perez was shoeing horses in Casey's corral and it was obvious that he would not be venturing far afield that day, so they set out to look for Hogan.

Cowdrey pointed to the high point of the timber-clad ridge that reared on their left. 'You know, Charley, if I was Hogan I'd use that place to spy out the lie of the land.'

His companion nodded. 'It's worth a look, but keep under cover. We don't want to get into a gunfight with Hogan.'

'I don't expect to find him there but we might be able to see if he's been there.'

'Let's keep under cover as we go up there. Ain't no use in setting ourselves up for an ambush.'

High on the ridge, Hogan could not see the two riders approaching. He was using the field glasses and concentrating on distant scenes, unaware of approaching danger.

TWELVE

It was a coyote that first warned Hogan. It came up the ridge looking over its shoulder and scarcely noticing the man and horse. Aware that frightened animals usually take an uphill course when running from danger, Hogan turned the glasses down the slope and readjusted the focus. The pines were too thick to see through so he put away the glasses and hung the case from his saddle horn. Reins in hand, he peered down through the greenery. He thought he saw movement but whatever it was disappeared again.

A sound carried upward and he recognized it as that of a large stone rolling downhill. Some large animal had displaced it and many times he had seen horses kick stones loose on steep slopes. Someone was below with horses. Quietly he led Diamond clear of the trees to mount. But before he could do so Winston's horse came bounding up the slope. Cowdrey's was a horse-length behind. Both riders halted in surprise.

With the advantage of prior warning, Hogan drew his gun before the others fully comprehended what had occurred. 'Keep your hands away from your guns.'

Neither man needed telling twice. This man had killed Ace Collins, a professional gunfighter.

'Don't shoot,' Cowdrey said. 'We ain't going for our guns.'

'Turn your horses side-on and get off this side. Don't try any tricks.'

As the men turned their mounts Hogan read the brands. 'A couple of Marryat's men, eh. What are you doing dogging my tracks?'

'We didn't know you were here,' Winston tried to sound convincing. 'We were out looking for strays.'

'Up here where there's no grass or water?'

'We figured we might see a few from up here.'

'What's happening with Templeman?'

'He gave up and went back to town. We ain't working for him, we're Marryat's hands.' Cowdrey tried to sound as though he spoke the truth.

' As far as I can tell Marryat and Templeman

are one and the same. Unbuckle your gun belts and step away from them and don't do anything stupid.'

Both men obeyed.

'Now, why exactly is Templeman after me?'

Winston answered nervously. 'He reckons you murdered Ace Collins and tried to kill Matt Pritchard.'

'Who brought the sheriff into this?' Hogan demanded.

'Marryat did. Ace's horse came home without him and when we backtracked we found Pritchard walking. He reckoned you ambushed him.'

Keeping a close eye on his prisoners, Hogan picked up their gun belts, buckled them again and hung them over the horns on their saddles. Then he knotted the reins and hooked them to the saddle horns. 'I hope you boys like walking,' he said and swatted the nearest horse on the rump with his hat. The startled animal took off at a gallop and the other one followed it.

The two cowhands looked on in horror.

'We're six miles from home and I have new boots,' Cowdrey protested.

Hogan showed him little sympathy. 'Think yourself lucky that you are still able to walk. You can pass the word around. I won't go so easy on the next people who get too close to me. You can tell your boss that Pritchard is a liar. I shot Ace Collins but he and Pritchard were both trying to kill me at the time. Now get walking and remember what I said.'

When he was sure that the cowhands were out of sight, Hogan rode down the other side of the slope, intending to check on his ranch and horses. Perez was checking periodically but he had some good saddle stock that might tempt some of the less scrupulous town elements. An unattended ranch was an opportunity that a few of them would not be able to resist. He kept under cover as much as he could but the last half-mile was over open country. If someone was watching the ranch he might have been riding into a trap, but he decided to take the risk.

The barn was the most obvious place for an enemy to wait so he approached from a side where there were no windows or doors. Fifty yards short of the building, he dismounted, hid his horse in a creek-bed and crept to the weathered back wall. Cautiously, with a cocked six-gun in his hand, he stepped around the corner. One of the double doors was opened. He had left both closed. He also knew that Perez would have closed any doors before leaving.

Hogan took a chance. He stepped quickly

around the door and into the gloomy building. No gun blasted at him and he knew he was alone. He was enjoying the sight and smell of the familiar building when he heard distant voices. Peering around the door, he saw two riders coming from the front gate.

At first he thought he had fallen into a trap, but then he recognized the riders. They were Walter Hill's two cowhands. Both had Winchesters in their hands and were looking about as though searching for some hidden danger. Hogan decided that he would not show himself too soon.

They halted near the barn.

He recognised Corbett's voice. 'I don't see any sign of the thieving coyote now but he was here. Must have took off when he saw me watching him. Probably some no-good helping himself to Ned's stuff when he knows he ain't here.'

'Did you get a good look at him?' Hynes asked.

'No, he looked sort of ordinary but he was riding a nice brown horse; looked like a Morgan to me.'

Aware that the men were not discussing him, Hogan decided to show himself. 'Howdy, boys. What's happening?'

Both men were totally surprised when

Hogan stepped out of the barn.

Hynes gaped for a second and said: 'Ned – where did you come from?'

'I live here. Remember?'

Corbett looked worried. 'Templeman was here the other day – he's looking everywhere for you. We thought that maybe one of his deputies might still be around here – either that or a thief.'

'Is there a difference?' Hogan asked.

The two cowhands told him that they were investigating a mysterious stranger whom Corbett had seen lurking about Hogan's barn that morning. The distance was too great to recognize the stranger but he knew that it was not Hogan or Perez.

'Nice to know that folks here are still looking after my interests. Let's have a look in the barn and see if there is anything missing.'

The dusty harness still hung on its pegs, tools were propped against the wall and the loft contained only hay. At first it seemed that nothing had been disturbed until Hogan noticed a gap in the line of bottles arranged on a shelf. The bottles were mostly various veterinary preparations. When he checked the shelf, a clean spot in the dust showed where a bottle had rested until very recently. Then he remembered. There had been a blue bottle in that position. It had contained poison.

'Looks like our visitor stole an old bottle of poison that I had here,' Hogan told the others.

'Maybe he was figuring to poison hisself,' Corbett suggested.

'Or someone else,' Hynes added.

'I should have been looking for tracks,' Hogan reproached himself. 'We have probably walked all over any that he left by now.'

After searching for a while they found a couple of boot-prints that had been made by flat-heeled boots.

'I think we are looking at the tracks of Henry Power,' Hogan announced at last.

Corbett looked blank. 'Who the hell is he?'

'He's a range detective hired by the big cattlemen to force small ranchers off their land and to murder them if they don't go. I'm sure this man killed your former boss.'

'Nick Meyers is our boss these days until the ranch is sold,' Hynes said. 'But he don't interfere too much.'

'Has he mentioned a prospective buyer?'

The cowhand shook his head. 'Not to us. He is one close-mouthed sonofabitch that way. He's a real professional lawyer and would bill you later if you asked him how to get out of a burning building. At present we ain't asking nothing and he's telling us nothing.'

Hogan retrieved his horse and the trio tracked the mysterious visitor to the ranch's front gate. He had crossed the road and his tracks eventually disappeared in rocky country.

'Looks like he's heading straight south over the Big Squaw Range and out of the valley,' Hynes said.

Hogan was not so sure. 'That's the opposite way to where I expected. It's the opposite way to Marryat's and he's the only rancher around here with enough money to hire Henry Power.'

Corbett had another idea. 'He could be doing this to throw us off the track. He might change direction later. But you shouldn't be seen with us, Ned. Templeman's sure to come sniffing around here again. We'll keep looking around and see what we find. How can we get in touch with you?'

'Tell Juán and he'll get word to me.'

'One thing's for sure,' Hynes said. 'That Power feller has to get closer to poison folks than he does to shoot them.'

Hogan turned his horse. 'Remember, boys, you haven't seen me. Thanks too for keeping an eye on my place.'

THIRTEEN

Power was a little uneasy. He had not counted on Hogan's nosy neighbours. Now someone else knew that a stranger was in the valley. He had been forced to make a wide detour to shake off any pursuit before turning back to his hideout. He knew that soon his employer would be demanding results. One dead and a family forced out had not frightened the other small ranchers. He could not find Hogan, so the next victim had to be Mike Casey. He felt the blue bottle in his coat pocket. With the dogs out of the way his chances would improve greatly.

Perez was a problem too. The man's daily checking of the immediate ranch house area was forcing him to keep at distances where accuracy could not be guaranteed. Power wondered how easy it would be to frighten Perez into discontinuing his patrols. Could he achieve his purpose by a wounding or a near miss?

Time was dragging for Hogan. The enforced idleness and the lack of friendly faces were a greater problem than he had previously realized. Sleeping out at a different location each night and eating cold meals quickly became onerous. He roamed the hills and carefully avoided any riders whom he saw. Templeman had not given up. He was sure of that.

With no particular destination in mind Hogan found himself on the high ground behind Casey's ranch. He took the field glasses and studied the buildings. A grey pony was standing saddled in the corral and it looked like Ellie's. Another, darker-coloured horse was also hitched to the rail. A flash of colour came into his field of view and he could discern the girl's red jacket. A taller person walked beside her; it could have been Dave, her elder brother. That was good he thought. She would not be riding around alone.

The two riders left the ranch and to Hogan's delight, they began to ride in his direction. Keeping under concealment as much as possible, he set Diamond on a course that would intercept the two Caseys.

The shock showed on their faces when they saw a rider emerge from around a large boulder about fifty yards ahead. Then recognition dawned.

'Howdy, folks, out for a ride?' Hogan asked.

'Ned, you look like a Mexican bandit,' Ellie laughed. 'We weren't expecting to see you here.'

'Sorry about the beard. Where are you off to?'

Her brother answered: 'Just riding about. We thought that we would see what we could see.'

'Have you seen any strangers about?'

'Not a one,' Ellie said. 'Tell us what you have been doing.'

'I will tonight,' Hogan promised. 'When it gets dark I'll visit your house. I have something important to tell you.'

'Should we tell any of the neighbours?' Dave asked. 'Sam Hockley is keen to organize our own posse and try to find this range detective. He's a bit worried that the killer will strike soon if we give him time to plan things.'

'Everything that murdering sonof—' He noted Ellie's glare and remembered just in time. 'Everything that killer does is very carefully planned, but tonight I aim to upset his little scheme.'

Dave became full of enthusiasm. 'Sounds like you know what he's going to do, Ned. Do you think we can lay a trap for him?'

'I'm only guessing, Dave, but I reckon that sometime in the next couple of nights you might have an unwelcome visitor.'

Ellie pointed to the little holstered .32 buckled around her slim waist. 'Let him come. I'll give him a hot reception if I see him.'

Her brother laughed. 'That little gun's bullets will bounce clear off him, Sis. You need something heavier.'

'At least I'll hit him. You will probably miss with that old .44 of yours. Is there anything we can get ready for you, Ned when you come tonight?'

'No, but thanks all the same. The food your mother's been sending out with Juán has been really good but I do miss my hot coffee. Living without a fire can get a bit tiresome. If all is clear for me to come in, get someone to walk past the back window of the kitchen twice, carrying a lamp. If I don't see that I'll figure that something is wrong. Remind your father, too, that he is still on the killer's list. Tell him not to make a target of himself.'

'Juán tells him that all the time. He looks after us like a sheepdog,' Ellie said.

'That's good. It's best you go home now and let your family know what I have told you. I'll see you tonight.'

*

101

Power selected his target with care. He could not shoot a calf in case the mother stayed nearby and attracted unwanted attention. He chose a young steer bearing Marryat's brand. It was feeding on the long grass at the edge of a dry creek-bed. He dismounted, unlimbered his rifle and killed the unfortunate animal with one shot to the forehead. It tumbled down the bank out of sight. Then he hitched his horse in the shelter of some willows, took a razor-sharp clasp-knife from his pocket and skinned back the steer's hide on a hindleg. Working swiftly he cut out a large piece of meat which he cut into six smaller pieces. Then he made a deep incision in each piece and sprinkled in the white powder he had taken from Hogan's barn. Last of all he wrapped the bloody gobbets in a piece of old sacking and placed the parcel in his saddle-bag.

If his plan worked another of Casey's defences would soon be gone; even if it failed it would increase the rancher's anxiety. There was always a chance that family pressures would force him to reconsider his decision to stay.

Power had never liked handling poison and the range detective halted at a secluded spot along Warbonnet Creek to clean his knife and thoroughly wash his hands. It would soon be dark, but he would have several hours before it was safe to put his plan into action. The night could be a long one, so Power decided to return to his hideout for a meal. He was a man who planned everything carefully, but with Hogan loose somewhere on the range Power was aware that his planning could go awry. Templeman had complicated the issue by forcing the rancher into hiding.

The range detective had built his reputation on efficient and quiet removal of his employers' enemies but to date the Warbonnet Creek operation was not going to plan. Hogan was the main problem. He had to be killed quickly before the smaller ranchers started to rally around him.

FOURTEEN

Hogan received a great reception when he arrived at Casey's that night. He was a little self-conscious about his unkempt appearance but Perez said that the problem could easily be rectified. The new clothes ordered from town had been delivered and a large tub of hot water was waiting for him in the bunkhouse. When Hogan returned to the ranch house, he felt greatly refreshed.

With the two Casey boys keeping guard outside he enjoyed a hot meal and discussed the situation with the others.

Casey frowned as Hogan told him what he had learned. 'So you think this Power character is planning to pay us a visit soon?'

'I'm almost sure of it. I think he took that poison to bait your dogs. Keep them tied up at night to make his job a little harder.'

Ellie asked: 'Could he be meaning to put it in our well?'

'There might not be enough when it is diluted by the amount of water there,' her mother said.

Hogan reminded them: 'He can't get to the well without going past the dogs. I think they are his main target. But we might be able to turn this to our advantage. For the first time we have an idea of what he is going to do.'

'But we don't know when he is going to do it,' Perez added.

'It could be tonight,' Hogan said. 'While I am here there is an extra gun, so why not set a trap tonight and see if he falls into it? Juán and I could hide outside where we could see anyone coming near the house.'

'But he could come from any direction,' Jean Casey said.

Hogan disagreed. 'He has to come downwind from the dogs. If we figure out how the breezes are blowing, we should have a good idea which direction to watch.'

They talked for another hour until Jean Casey mentioned that it was getting near their usual bedtime. Hogan suggested that the killer might have studied their daily routines and that he might become suspicious if the lamps stayed on longer than usual. Reluctantly he decided that it was time to take up his position outside.

Power was watching from the ridge. One by one he saw the lights snuffed out at the ranch house. Though impatient to start his task he forced himself to wait. He wanted everyone asleep before he ventured near the buildings. Cutting another piece from his plug of chewing-tobacco, he seated himself on a rock and waited.

An hour later he checked the wind direction. He would have to do a wide half-circle around the buildings and approach from the front. He knew that there were three dogs chained only a few yards apart. Once he was close enough to the animals he did not care if they barked. He would throw them the baits and flee. Before any of the Caseys could investigate the dogs would have gulped down fatal doses of poison.

Hogan and Perez concealed themselves about fifty yards apart on the downwind side of the dogs and settled down to wait. The night was moonless and visibility was poor. There was never complete silence: night birds called, the dogs stirred and occasionally some small animal could be heard scurrying through the grass.

Hogan guessed that an hour had dragged by when he heard something different. He was not sure what it was but it did not fit in with the normal night sounds. He listened. A few seconds later it came again.

A dog-chain rattled and he heard a low growl. At least one of the dogs had heard the sound too, but was curious because there was no scent. Hogan eased his gun from its holster.

Suddenly the light patter of feet came out of the darkness and a vague shape hurried forward. The dogs began to bark.

Hogan cocked his gun. 'Put your hands up.'

Caught in the act of throwing the baits to the dogs, Power dropped them and drew his gun. Hogan saw the movement and fired. A gun roared and a red muzzle-flash came back at him. In such bad light both shooters missed but both tried again. Perez also tried a long-range shot at the intruder's muzzle flash. Someone fired too from the front window of the house.

Power turned and ran. The odds were too great for him even to consider continuing the fight.

His opponents could hear him but could not see him.

Hogan yelled: 'Let's get him, Juán.' Then, as he ran forward, he tripped on an unseen stone and went sprawling.

Perez heard the fall. 'Are you OK, Ned?'

'I'm fine. Don't let him get away.'

The half-breed heard the sound of a horse and the squeak of leather as Power threw himself into the saddle. Unable to get within effective range, he emptied his gun in the general direction as the rider galloped away.

Something burned along the side of his right lower leg but the range detective ignored it. Trusting to his horse's night vision, he spurred headlong into the darkness.

Hogan ran to the barn where he had left his saddled horse. Seconds later he was in the saddle. As he galloped past Perez the half-breed called: 'He's turned left out of the front gate.'

Power heard another horse behind him but he had a good lead and was sure that he could shake off the pursuit in the darkness. His leg was beginning to hurt but he dared not stop to examine the wound. There would be time for that later. At a dark clump of trees in the shadow of a hill, he reined in his horse and turned off the trail. Then he drew his revolver and waited.

Hogan could only follow the sound of the other horse and this was being drowned out by the beat of his own mount's hoofs. Reluctantly he stopped his horse and listened. He heard nothing. Power was nearby. He knew that much, but trying to find him in the darkness was only asking to be ambushed. He had actually ridden a hundred yards past where Power was hiding. When he decided to abandon the chase, he rode back past Power's concealment again but the gunman was not close enough for an accurate shot in such poor light and so held his fire.

The drumming of galloping hoofs announced the arrival of other riders. Juán and Casey had mounted horses bareback and followed the direction that Hogan had taken.

He called: 'Over here.' The riders found him in the slightly lighter area out of the shadows of the trees.

'Did you get him?' Casey asked as he drew abreast with Hogan.

'No, he got away in the dark.'

'Horses coming,' Perez said urgently.

'They might not be on our side. Be careful,' Hogan warned.

The riders were galloping straight up the road. There were two of them both riding at reckless speed.

Hogan drew his revolver and tried to remember the number of shots he had already fired. He rode his horse out into the middle of the road where the oncoming riders could see him. Both checked their horses and slowed them before halting a few yards from the rancher.

'Who's that?'

Hogan recognized the voice of Sam Hockley. 'Ned Hogan, Sam. Did you pass anyone else on the road?'

'No, what happened?'

'Someone visited Casey's tonight and we swapped a few shots.' As Hogan spoke Casey and Perez rose out of the ambush positions they had taken up.

'Was anyone hurt?' Hockley asked. 'Wilt Norris and I both heard the shooting and reckoned that we might be needed.'

'We nearly got him,' Casey said, 'but shooting in the dark is mostly a matter of luck. We'll get him next time.'

Hockley asked: 'Who are you talking about, Mike?'

'That range detective, Henry Power. He was seen this morning at Hogan's by one of Walter Hill's men. And the murdering sonofabitch is hiding out somewhere around here.'

'It seems to me,' Hockley told them, 'that we should organize a posse and make a big sweep right through this area.'

'It's a big area to try to cover,' Hogan said. 'I doubt we could raise enough men.'

Casey disagreed. 'It might give Power a good

scare and frighten him out of the area. We could even force Templeman into it.'

'Who needs him?' Hogan growled. 'We want all our enemies out in front of us. He would only work against us. He's a friend of Power's.'

'I wonder if he would stay a friend if Power was to prove an embarrassment,' Hockley ventured. 'Templeman has a nice little job there and would not want to lose it. We could worry him by forcing him to get involved in a situation he is trying hard to avoid. It would be nice to see him squirming.'

Casey chuckled. 'He would need Marryat's permission just to squirm.'

While the horsemen sat in the middle of the road arguing, Henry Power quietly rode wide of them and continued on his way to his hideout. His leg was hurting and he needed to dress the wound.

FIFTEEN

Hogan did not return to Casey's. He had achieved his main purpose in frustrating Power's attempt and would not become involved in the posse that Hockley was raising. His presence would be enough to put them on the wrong side of the law. Templeman would like nothing better than to discredit the small ranchers. It had been a long day and he was very tired. He rode to the nearest of his hide-outs, a place roofed over by an enormous slab of rock and screened from view by a clump of cedars. By peering through the trees he could overlook several miles of country along Warbonnet Creek.

He picketed his horse and fed it some of the oats that he had brought from Casey's. Then, using a slicker for a groundsheet, he stretched out nearby, his head cushioned on his saddle-bags and a sweaty saddle blanket over him.

He arose around sun-up and made a hurried breakfast on some of the food packed for him by Jean Casey. Tasty though it was, he remembered the hot meal of the previous night and wondered how long it would be before he had another such repast.

Perez had risen early too. He had found the dog baits that Power had dropped and he searched around for tracks. The odd print of a flat-heeled boot confirmed that they had traded shots with Power and he found them going and coming to where the killer had concealed his horse. He was following the horse tracks when he noticed what appeared to be dried blood on a nearby stone. A little further beyond the front gate he found another suspicious drop, but no other positive clues. The riders coming and going through the night had ridden over the killer's horse's tracks and he knew that it would be useless trying to pick them up again.

Ellie had been washing the dirty clothes that Hogan had left behind and was hanging them on the clothes'-line when the half-breed came back to the yard behind the house. 'Did you find anything, Juán?' she asked.

'I saw where he left his horse. There was

nothing unusual about its tracks. We mostly covered them up riding around last night in the dark. But there is a chance that someone might have wounded Power or his horse. I saw what looked like a couple of spots of dried blood. There wasn't much of it but last night we might have had some luck.'

'What if the blood was from his horse?'

'A horse is a big strong animal, Miss Ellie, and it has to be hit just right with a six-gun to stop it in its tracks. I've seen horses shot in Indian fights and their riders never knew it until they were unsaddling later. They were stiff and sore for a few days but most of them got right.'

'So there is most likely a wounded horse or a wounded rider around somewhere. Ned should be told of this. Will you take me to him?'

'Now hold on there. Your folks might have something to say about that.'

'I told them I was going for a ride today and they know I'm safe with you. Just wait there, Juán, until I change into my riding-clothes.'

'Ned might not like this, Miss Ellie.'

She smiled. 'Do you mean that he would not want to see me?'

'Sure, he would like to see you more than anyone else I can think of but he would not like to see you in danger.'

Ellie laughed. 'There's no danger, Juán. You will be with me.'

Perez shook his head doubtfully.

Hogan was sprawled bellydown on a hill with his field glasses, watching the distant shapes of riders. There were four of them and they came from the direction of Marryat's ranch. They seemed to be inspecting the range cattle, occasionally rounding up small bunches, looking them over and moving on.

As they moved closer he was able to distinguish a small man on a big horse: Marryat. One rider stayed at the little rancher's side and did not participate in the cattle work. Hogan was sure that that would be Pritchard, the hired gun. His presence added a sinister aspect to what otherwise would have been a normal scene on the range.

Marryat was a good cattleman and tried not to disturb the grazing cattle unduly as he inspected them. That was a reassuring sight to Hogan, as it was obvious that the riders were not hunting him.

From his elevated position he could see both sides of a low hill but did not notice the other pair of riders until it was already too late. His heart jumped when he suddenly recognized

Ellie's grey pony and the lean figure of Perez beside her. They appeared to be making for the place where he had camped for the night. But they were also on a collision course with Marryat and his men. At that stage neither party could see the other but the situation would soon change.

Hogan put away the glasses and ran to his horse. He had no plan in mind other than to get on the scene as quickly as possible. Ellie and Juan were both in great danger.

'Well, look here,' Pritchard pointed ahead. 'It's that Casey girl and Hogan's 'breed friend. She ain't fussy about the company she keeps.'

Too late, Perez saw the others. They had been concealed by a patch of standing timber. 'I'll hold them here, Miss Ellie. Run for home – now.'

'No, Juán,' Ellie said. 'I don't want you being killed. We must try to talk our way out of this. I've done nothing against Mr Marryat.'

'That Pritchard with him is a very bad man. He is sure to start trouble.'

'I'm staying. Let's ride over and see what they want.'

'Keep an eye on that 'breed,' Marryat whispered to Pritchard as the two riders approached. 'You're a long way from home,

Miss Casey,' he greeted.

'No further from home than you are, Mr Marryat. I seem to recall that this is public land. Juán and I are looking at the cattle. Someone has to a keep an eye on Ned's stock while he's not around.'

Marryat chuckled. 'Get used to him not being around. He's a rustler and a murderer and it's only a matter of time before the law catches up with him.'

'Just on the subject of murderers, your hired murderer paid us a visit last night and got a very hot reception. Has he told you about that yet?'

A puzzled look came across the rancher's face. He looked at Pritchard but the gunman shook his head. 'What are you talking about, Miss Casey?'

'You know. You are the only one around here who can afford to hire gunmen.'

'I assure you that I don't know. I only hired Pritchard here after threats on my life. I make no secret of the fact that I consider there are too many rustlers among you small ranchers, but I would never have a man murdered.'

'I suppose you didn't order your men to burn Hogan's ranch house either.'

'You are right. I did not.'

'And you did not send Ace Collins and this

man here to kill Ned Hogan in Muddy Creek?'

Pritchard cut in savagely. 'That's a lie. Hogan bushwhacked us on our way back from town. Sheriff Templeman knows that.'

'Templeman only knows what he's told to know by you, Mr Marryat.'

The rancher protested his innocence. 'I don't—'

Pritchard rasped, 'Shut your lying mouth, girl, or I'll shut it for you.'

Perez moved his horse another length ahead of Ellie's. 'I think you had better mind your manners, Mr Pritchard.'

The gunman had achieved his purpose in diverting the conversation away from what he was anxious to hide. He smiled a cruel smile. 'You, a dirty 'breed lecturing a white man like me on manners. I'm going to enjoy shooting you.'

'That may be,' Perez said quietly, 'but I'll live long enough to put a bullet in you.'

Ellie ranged her pony beside Perez. 'And so will I.' Her hand was hovering over the butt of her gun. She looked nervous but determined.

'Stop this,' Marryat said, and steered his horse between the would-be combatants. But no chivalry or altruism prompted his actions. He knew that the death of a young girl would turn public opinion against him and even his

118

most influential friends would abandon him.

'Get out of the way, Marryat. I ain't listening to any more lies. If this stupid little bitch gets caught in the crossfire it will be her own fault.'

SIXTEEN

Hogan came spurring along the ridge, drawing his Winchester as he came. He took in the scene and got within fifty yards before the others noticed him.

'Pritchard!' He pulled Diamond to a sliding stop. 'Don't touch your gun.'

The gunman turned his mount to face a far more serious menace, but he wisely kept his hand clear of his gun. 'So you stopped hiding at last, Hogan. I've waited for this for a long time. Step down off that horse and we'll settle this matter now.'

'I'm happy where I am. If you want to start something, start it now.'

'But you have the drop on me.'

'And I intend to keep it on you but that shouldn't worry a big-time *pistolero* like you. Go for that gun any time you feel like it. You never know your luck and you have a couple of friends behind you.'

'I ain't involved in this,' one of Marryat's cowhands protested as he backed his horse away from Pritchard's.

The gunman considered his chances. What was a long and difficult shot for a revolver was easy for a man with a rifle. Pritchard was fully aware that he had built his reputation against men who were at close range and usually unprepared. He had a good chance against Perez with his tight horseman's holster, but against a Winchester the outlook was not so predictable. If he could narrow the gap between them he could turn the tables. He drove home his spurs and turned his horse straight at Hogan.

Resisting the urge to shoot too soon, the rancher took careful aim. Pritchard had drawn his gun and was raising it to fire when Hogan squeezed the trigger. The bullet's impact smashed Pritchard's right forearm and sent his revolver spinning through the air. The gunman tried to stop his horse but to his horror it carried him straight at Hogan. The latter levered a fresh cartridge into the breech, ready to shoot again if necessary.

'No!' Pritchard screamed. An arm bent at a wrong angle showed that he was no longer holding a gun.

Hogan lowered his rifle and slashed at the wounded gunman with the barrel as his horse raced past. Already unbalanced and in shock, Pritchard rolled back out of his saddle and crashed to the ground. The watchers saw his right arm flapping awkwardly as he rolled on the ground.

Aware that Pritchard was out of action, the rancher pointed his rifle at Marryat and his men. 'Anyone else want to join in?'

'We are not involved in this Hogan. We are not gunmen.'

'Neither am I, Marryat. Now what story are you going to tell your pet sheriff about this?'

'As far as I am concerned, it was a fair fight. I won't be making any complaint. What Pritchard does later is up to him.' Turning to his men the little rancher said: 'See what you can do for Pritchard. I'm returning to the ranch for a buckboard and to try to organize some medical help.'

Without taking his eyes from the others Hogan said to Ellie and Perez: 'Head for home. I'll catch up with you when I'm sure that nobody is planning to shoot us in the back.'

Ellie wanted to stay but Perez grabbed her pony's bridle. 'Do as he says, Miss Ellie. I don't want to come that close to dying again.'

A short while later Hogan galloped up to

them. He was still pale-faced and shaken by what had happened. 'Ellie,' he demanded, 'what in the blue blazes were you doing out here? You nearly got caught in a gunfight. What is so all-fired important to bring you out here where it is all so dangerous?'

'We wanted to tell you. Last night either that range detective or his horse was shot. Juan found the blood-drops this morning.'

'It was not a trail good enough to follow,' Perez explained, 'but we know now that somewhere along Warbonnet Creek there is a wounded man or horse. Who knows what they might find when Hockley gets a posse turning the place upside down?'

'I'm glad you didn't kill that man, Ned,' Ellie said. 'It was good that you only shot to wound him.'

'Actually, Ellie, I shot to kill. It was just a bad shot and I came close to missing him altogether. With any luck, though, he's finished as a gunman. There's no such thing as a minor wound when a big lead bullet hits bone. Even if he doesn't lose his arm, I doubt that he'll have the full use of it again.'

'I am very pleased to hear that,' Perez said. 'He could be a bad enemy in future. You arrived just in time, Ned. The best I could hope to do was to put a slug in him before I went.'

Ellie smiled and patted the half-breed's shoulder. 'He's a hero, Ned. You should have seen the way he stood up to Pritchard.'

Perez laughed. 'I had you backing me up. We had him outnumbered.'

Hogan did not join in the laughter. He knew how close he had come to losing his two best friends.

They returned to Casey's and told the family of the latest developments. Ellie's parents were horrified at their daughter's brush with death. Her two brothers were disappointed that they had missed out on the excitement.

Tom Casey chuckled. 'I would love to have seen the look on Marryat's face when his prize gunfighter was shot off his horse.'

'You'll be getting quite a reputation, Ned,' Dave Casey told the rancher. 'That's two *pistoleros* you've fixed now.'

'That's not the sort of reputation I want, Dave. Neither was a fair fight. I cheat.'

'Damn glad you did,' Mike Casey said and for once his wife did not reproach him for his profanity.

Later that day Sam Hockley arrived. He had been travelling around the small ranches, raising a posse. Their aim was to scour the valley of Warbonnet Creek and hunt down Henry Power. A secondary objective was to find a wounded or dead horse in the hope that it would provide a clue to its rider's whereabouts. The posse would split into four-man groups and would work scattered around the valley. Hockley's plan was that the fugitive, seeking to avoid one group, might run into the path of another.

Hogan suggested that they advise Marryat of the situation in the hope that he might contribute a couple of men. The idea was not warmly received and it was pointed out that the rancher had added to the problems with his imported gunmen. Others were not sure that he could be trusted. After all, he was the only rancher in the district who could afford a range detective's wages.

Then there was the question of Sheriff Templeman. Hogan was adamant that he should not be told of the ranchers' posse. 'He's known to be in cahoots with Power. He'll work against you if he's asked to help. Don't bring him into this.'

'Won't Marryat advise him of the posse?' Hockley asked.

'Even if he does, it will be too late,' Hogan replied.

'Will you be riding with us?' Casey asked Hogan.

'No, I don't want to compromise the posse. It

can hardly be classed as a group of law-abiding citizens if you have a wanted man riding with you. It's important that you keep within the law as much as possible. I have a few ideas of my own that I want to try out and the less others are involved the better.'

'That all sounds very mysterious,' Casey observed quietly. 'Why do I get the impression that you are going to do something not quite legal?'

'The way the law has been enforced around here, Mike, has left a lot to be desired. I might even get a bit of expert advice on the subject.'

'Sounds like you might be having a word with Nick Meyers in town.'

'Does it?'

'Be very careful around Muddy Creek, Ned. You might not have many friends there.'

SEVENTEEN

Hogan timed his visit to reach Muddy Creek around 4 p.m. He knew that the businesses in the sleepy little town would be preparing to close for the night. Those living nearby who might patronize the saloon would not yet be ready to venture into town. He fully intended to break the law, and the fewer witnesses the better.

Templeman would be resting before coming back on duty when night fell. He had no fear of the sheriff, but the man could cause added complications to what promised to be a tricky situation.

Hogan hitched his horse to the rail in front of the lawyer's office and entered the building quickly. He had hoped that the lawyer would be alone but found Gladys Staeder working in the outer office. A middle-aged widow, Gladys occasionally helped out with filing and some general office work.

'Howdy, Mrs Staeder. Is there anyone in with Mr Meyers at present?'

Recognition dawned but she covered it quickly. 'There's nobody there at present, but he might not be able to see you.'

'He'll see me,' Hogan said as he strode to the door of the lawyer's office. He knocked briefly and pushed it open.

Meyers looked up startled from his writing. His eyes behind the wire-framed spectacles widened in surprise. Then he put down his pen, pushed back his chair and indicated that Hogan should take a seat in the vacant chair on the other side of his broad, cluttered desk. Seeing the worried lady standing at the office doorway he said: 'Everything's fine, Gladys. You can finish up now.'

He waited until the door was closed, then said to Hogan: 'I have been expecting you. I presume that you want me to defend you over this affair with the late Ace Collins.'

'If it gets to court, I want you to represent me, but at present I'm here to ask a few questions about a few people.'

'Before we go any further, Mr Hogan, I suggest that you draw your gun and point it at me.'

'Now why would I want to do that?'

'Because I think that you are going to ask me about some of my other clients' business. Under normal circumstances I must refuse but when I am threatened by a gun the situation could change dramatically. Do you see my point?'

Hogan drew his gun but did not cock it. 'I think I see what you're driving at.'

'What do you want to know?'

'Has anyone made an offer for the Bohm ranch?'

'Yes.'

'And Walter Hill's place?'

'Yes.'

'Did any offers come from Marryat?'

'No, he made no offers on those ranches. In fact he sounded out with me the idea of selling out himself.'

This news took Hogan completely by surprise. 'You are telling me the truth?'

Meyers allowed himself a rare smile. 'Would a man in fear of his life risk giving a wrong answer?'

'Has the same person offered to buy both ranches?'

'It is not a person but a company: the West Texas Cattle Company, to be exact. It is a consortium of Texas cattle barons.'

'So they're the ones who hired Henry Power,

the range detective?'

'I can't say that for sure because nothing of that nature has ever been disclosed to me.'

'Where can I find the man who is representing them?'

Again Meyers gave a tight little smile. 'I suggest you look in your own neighbourhood. He lives in the Warbonnet Creek valley. His name is Samuel Hockley.'

Hogan was stunned by the news. 'But he's a small rancher like the rest of us.'

'I'm afraid he is not. He is merely a front man for the West Texas Cattle Company. I am glad that you held me up and forced this information out of me. I have heard about the trouble along Warbonnet Creek, but the rules of my profession prohibited me from telling what I knew.'

Hogan arose and holstered his gun. 'I can't thank you enough for what you have told me.'

'Remember,' said the lawyer. 'I volunteered nothing. It was all forced out of me at gunpoint.' He extended a hand. 'Good luck, Mr Hogan. I don't think there is any case against you over the Collins shooting but I will represent you if there is.'

The rancher thanked Meyers profoundly and stepped out onto the boardwalk, to come face to face with a very surprised Sheriff Templeman.

It was a confrontation that neither wanted and for an instant each stared at the other, but Hogan reacted slightly faster. He had his gun out before the sheriff even dragged his coat clear from the grip of his weapon.

For one second Templeman thought he was going to die. There was panic in his eyes and his mouth hung open.

'Don't move,' Hogan snapped at him.

'I'm not moving. Don't shoot.'

The rancher looked about and saw no one on the street. 'You're just the man I wanted to see, Sheriff. Is there anyone in your office?'

'No. My deputy's away at present.'

'That's good. We are going to take a walk down there and have a little talk. You have no idea how much I am going to enjoy this little conversation. Now get walking and don't do anything hasty.'

When they reached the sheriff's office, Templeman unlocked the door and both men entered. By this time the sheriff had regained some of his composure. 'You won't get away with this,' he threatened as his gun was plucked from its holster.

'At present my chances are better than yours. Now just stand still while I frisk you. You're sure to have a hideout gun somewhere.'

Hogan was right. He found a short-barrelled

.38 in a shoulder holster. He threw the weapon on Templeman's desk. 'Now take a seat,' he ordered, 'and tell me all about Henry Power.'

'Don't know him.'

Hogan had been expecting such an answer. 'You're lying, Templeman.'

He produced a pair of handcuffs from the top drawer of the sheriff's desk. 'Lock this around one wrist.'

'I wo—'

Hogan backhanded him across the mouth. 'You were saying?'

Defeated, the sheriff obeyed. At his captor's urging he walked to the cell area at the back of the building.

'Now lock that cuff around the bar of that cell.'

Licking his split lips, Templeman did as he was told.

'Now did I hear you right? You really don't know Power?'

'Go to hell, Hogan.'

'I think you are going to get there first, my lying friend. I'll be right back. Don't run away.'

Hogan returned with a lamp. He splashed the oil out of it onto the floor and onto Templeman. 'Alive and not talking, you're no use to anyone,' he said. 'Looks like there's going to be a new sheriff's office needed here. I doubt you'll be missed, though.' He produced a box of matches from his pocket and selected one.

Templeman cracked. At first terror robbed him of his voice but on the second try, he croaked: 'I'll talk. Don't do this. I'll talk.'

Hogan made no attempt to put the matches away. 'I'll just keep these handy. The first lie you tell will also be your last. Do you understand?'

'I'll tell you anything you want to know. Will you let me go then?'

'I will on condition that you get to hell out of Muddy Creek and don't come back. You branded me a killer so I have nothing to lose by putting daylight through you. Now let's have a little talk.'

EIGHTEEN

Henry Power tested his wounded leg and winced in pain but found that he could walk on it. His confidence had taken a battering. So much had gone wrong with his Warbonnet Creek operations. Normally he would have shot a few people and had the rest in a state of panic but to date he had only earned $500 for the shooting of Walter Hill. His employers were ruthless people and they expected results. If he failed them he could well become a target himself. He knew too much and was tied to his employers. They would never allow him to tell what he knew.

Safely from his hiding-place at Hockley's ranch he had seen the posse assemble and noted the directions in which they were sent. Hockley was a smart one, he knew. He had arranged for certain areas to be searched first so that they would be safe for Power to travel through later. The range detective had a crucial task that day. Hogan had gone to town looking for answers and must never be allowed back into the Warbonnet Creek valley.

Having checked his surroundings from under cover, Power limped out through the back door and made his way to a small corral where Hockley had left a horse for him. Saddling the animal was easy enough but mounting presented a problem. He could not take the weight on his right leg to get the left foot in the stirrup. Eventually he had to lead the horse to the front of the house and mount from the veranda steps. Riding was far from comfortable because he could not put much weight in the off-side stirrup but the range detective forced himself to keep going.

Aware that the eastern end of the valley had already been searched, he rode directly to the bordering ridges. The tracks of possemen showed clearly on the ground in places. And once he sighted a small group of riders far to the west. They had already passed where Power wanted to be. He was beginning to think that his luck might have changed for the better.

Hockley had told him that Hogan had gone to Muddy Creek and now he was familiar enough with the country to know the route that his intended target would take on the way home. The rancher always went cross-country through the open range.

Power selected a spot that gave him a good view into a clear valley. He found a good shooting position but was forced to conceal his horse a hundred yards away in a clump of trees. After securing the animal, he had a difficult journey back to the chosen spot. The hillside was littered with fist-sized, round rocks, probably blown there by a volcanic explosion thousands of years before. It was tricky walking for a man with two good legs, and the range detective fell over several times before reaching his destination. On the last fall the rifle fell from his grasp and clattered down the rocks before coming to a halt a few feet further down the hill. He struggled down to it, picked it up and checked the weapon for damage. He found a few dents and scratches on the stock and cursed silently as he saw that a stone had gouged through the bluing to expose raw metal on the upper part of the barrel. Power had always been careful about his rifle and the latest mishap did nothing to improve his temper. Brushing the loose dust off with his sleeve he positioned himself behind a bush and sat down to wait.

Hogan listened eagerly as Templeman responded to his questions. The sheriff confessed that he knew Henry Power and knew of his business in Warbonnet Creek. He had been paid a substantial bribe by the West Texas Cattle Company to ignore what would happen when the range detective went to work.

'You mean that you took a bribe to condone murder?' Hogan demanded.

The sheriff said lamely: 'There was a rustling problem. He was only cleaning out rustlers.'

'There was no rustling problem and how in the hell would that company know if there was. They had only just arrived. Now what was Marryat's role in all this?'

'He had nothing to do with the killings. He used to pay me to investigate claims of rustling to worry the small ranchers and keep them honest. He knew nothing about Power.'

'Then he was on Power's death list too?'

'No, the note was only meant to frighten him into doing something extreme, like hiring gunmen.'

'Well, that certainly worked. Now I'm going to get Nick Meyers and you are going to repeat what you told me to him.'

'I won't do that. I'll be ruined.'

'Then there's no point in me keeping you alive. I know enough now to fix things without you.' Hogan produced a match as he spoke.

Templeman went white with fear. 'No – don't do that. I'll talk to Meyers.'

Half an hour later the ashen-faced sheriff signed the confession he had dictated to the lawyer. The lawyer shook his head and took Hogan to one side. 'This confession was obtained under duress. It won't stand up in court.'

'Who cares? Templeman is very badly frightened and as soon as I let him go, he'll hot-foot it out of town if he has any sense. I'm going home now. Show that confession to a few more of the town's citizens and then let Templeman go. He won't give you any more trouble.'

Hogan delayed his departure only long enough to tell Muddy Creek's newly resigned sheriff that he would shoot him on sight if their paths ever crossed again. Then he mounted his horse and set out for Warbonnet Creek.

Power's mood had not improved. His wounded leg throbbed and he was getting sore from the pumpkin-sized rock he had chosen for a seat.

His good leg was getting cramped and he stretched it sideways out from under the sheltering bush as he waited.

When he raised his rifle to his shoulder to check the sights, he saw a gleam of bare metal where a stone had chipped the blue from the shoulder of the rear sight. The shiny metal disturbed his sight picture and he knew that it could affect his accuracy at long range. Taking a match from his pocket, he struck it and held it over the sight until it was black again.

He looked up as he finished his task and saw the distant figure of a horseman. Hogan had just ridden into view. Hurriedly he struggled around to a more comfortable position and lined up his sights on the rider.

NINETEEN

Hogan's gaze was attracted by the sudden blaze of the match against the dark green of the bush. It was a long way off and he was not sure what it was, but then he caught the movement as Power withdrew his leg behind the bush. Though unsure of the true situation he became aware that something different was ahead and, given the recent events, he was in no mood to take chances. He touched his mount with the spurs and changed course, heading for a point from where he could see behind the bush while keeping at long range.

Power knew that his target had been alerted and struggled around to sight on Hogan as the latter rode wide on his right. The ground was rough and the horse was constantly changing its pace and direction. Even as he sighted and squeezed the trigger, the range detective knew that he had missed.

The bullet buzzed close to Hogan's ear and he saw the powder smoke drifting from behind the bush. A few more strides by his horse took him into a position where he could see a man in a brown coat raising his rifle again for another shot. He turned the horse downhill and the bullet raised a cloud of dust from the hillside above him.

Hampered by his injured leg, Power could not turn fast enough to get another shot at the tiny figure of the horseman galloping past on his right. Soon Hogan would be in a position to see him clearly and could command his escape route back to his horse. Power was no coward, but he had always left himself a means of retreat. For the first time in his career his retreat was cut off. He flicked open the breech and fed in another big cartridge. With his body twisted awkwardly in an attempt to follow his target, he fired again.

Hogan's horse shied as the bullet buzzed past its head. The rancher could see Power clearly by then and noted that the range detective had little in the way of cover. Obviously he had not expected a prolonged exchange of fire. As there were plenty of boulders on Hogan's side of the shallow valley, and he was in carbine range, he decided to take the fight to his opponent. He drew his Winchester from the

141

saddle boot, checked his mount, jumped from the saddle and took cover behind a rock.

The range detective, aware of his exposed position, stretched full length on the ground and took what shelter he could behind the small rock that previously he had been using as a seat. He fired and stung Hogan's face with tiny stone chips from a near miss as the rancher peered from shelter.

With his enemy using a single-shot rifle, Hogan had time to fire three rapid shots from his repeater before the return fire came again. The big lead bullet smacked solidly against his rocky protection before whining off in a ricochet. There was a bigger boulder a few yards away and the rancher sprinted for it while Power reloaded. He only just reached cover before the next shot. The range detective could reload and fire quicker than most men.

Hogan was beginning to regret his decision to dismount. He could not understand why Power had remained in such an exposed position, but he was having trouble taking advantage of the situation. Every time he showed himself a well-directed bullet came his way. He was up against a very skilled marksman and could not afford to be careless. He had little option but to work closer to his man to improve his own chances of scoring a hit. Timing his runs between Power's shots, he moved from boulder to boulder and narrowed the distance between them to a hundred yards.

The range detective had plenty of ammunition and was prepared to use it. He fired several shots that he knew would miss but would go close enough to cause his enemy a few doubts about his own chances. He would try to panic Hogan into a rash move that would leave him momentarily exposed.

He fired and flipped open the rifle's breech. The brass base of the cartridge came a slight distance out and stuck. The shell had cracked around the base and the extractor had simply torn through rather than dragging the empty shell from the chamber. Power stared in horror. Gently he took the still-hot base of the shell and tried to pull it clear. The end of the shell broke free in his hand but the rest of it was stuck fast in the rifle's firing-chamber. He had heard that when Springfield rifles became hot from rapid fire with high powered ammunition, the thin brass of the cartridge cases sometimes failed. But this was the first time that he had seen it. With his rifle out of action, virtually no cover, and an injured leg that hampered his movements Henry Power was rapidly running out of options. He would never surrender and now he decided upon a desperate gamble.

The next time a return shot from Hogan hit the rock near his head he lurched to his knees and dropped the rifle before pitching face down on the hillside.

The rancher saw his opponent's rifle fall from his hands and breathed a sigh of relief. Whether dead or seriously wounded, the fallen range detective no longer seemed to be a threat. Very cautiously, Hogan crossed the hollow and began to walk up the slope toward the inert figure. He too had a little trouble with the loose rocks because he dared not take his eyes off the form on the ground. Fifty yards short of the body he paused again and watched for any signs of life.

Power lay still, his right hand beneath his body clutching the revolver he had drawn as he fell. He dared not move and listened intently so that he would know when Hogan was in range. The sounds were getting closer.

'Power,' Hogan called. 'Can you hear me?'

No answer.

Convinced that the range detective was dead, he relaxed, set the hammer of his carbine on half-cock, and moved closer. Seeing the Springfield rifle lying on the ground with its long breechblock hanging open, he glanced at it, transferred his own rifle to his left hand and picked up the weapon.

At that instant Power suddenly became alive. He rolled sideways bringing his revolver up as he moved.

As a reflex action, Hogan speared the useless rifle straight into its owner's face.

Power ignored the pain as the barrel hit him in the mouth and concentrated all his efforts on getting his shot away.

Hogan drew his Colt as the menacing black bore of the range detective's gun swung in his direction. At that moment he slipped on the loose rock and fell to his knees.

Power fired and missed.

Hogan fired back and saw his target shudder as the bullet struck home.

Whether the range detective felt the bullet or the shock had not yet registered, he gave no indication of being seriously wounded. Instead he snapped his gun down for another shot.

Both men fired together and Hogan felt the hat lifted from his head. His own bullet caught Power at the base of the throat, toppling the man backwards, then his body rolled limply down the slope, leaving the six-gun on the stones behind him. This time there was no doubt. Henry Power's career of murder was over.

Hogan paused a while trying to gather his thoughts and wondering at his luck. He knew the situation might have been reversed if Power's rifle had remained in action.

A search of the dead man's pockets revealed little except a fat wallet, a pocket-knife, matches and some chewing-tobacco. A hundred yards away there was a stand of timber and there he found Power's horse. He unhitched it, mounted the animal and rode back across the hollow to where his own horse was quietly cropping the grass. There he changed mounts and rode back to the body.

It was no easy task lifting the limp body across the saddle and he was panting by the time he had secured the corpse in place. Then he mounted again and, leading Power's horse, set a course for Warbonnet Creek. His spirits lifted as he rode because now he knew who his enemies were and, more important, he knew where to find them.

It was dark when he reached Walter Hill's ranch and Hynes and Corbett were preparing an evening meal. When Hogan called them to the door and they saw the body on the horse, Hynes said: 'Don't tell me that murdering sonofabitch got someone else while we were out hunting for him.'

'This is Henry Power. He won't murder anyone else. He was aiming to dry-gulch me on the way back from town but his luck ran out.'

Corbett brought a lamp and looked at the dead man's face. 'So that's Henry Power. He don't look nothing special, does he?'

'He never was special,' Hynes muttered. 'Just a low-down skunk who murdered honest people. We rode all round the Warbonnet valley today looking for him and never saw hide nor hair of him.'

'You weren't supposed to. Sam Hockley is a front man for the same people who employed Power. He was leading you around so that Power could ambush me. He knew I was going to town and was probably frightened of what I might find there.'

'But Hockley's a small rancher,' Corbett protested. 'He wouldn't be working for the big cattle barons.'

'He works for the ones behind all this trouble, an outfit called the West Texas Cattle Company. I had a word with Meyers in town today; and Templeton confirmed that.'

'I wouldn't believe that lying coyote.' Corbett declared.

Hogan explained. 'For once in his life he told the truth and signed a confession to that effect. In return for being turned loose, the sheriff should by now be out of Muddy Creek, and you can bet that he has no intention of returning. Now, I'm going to collect a couple of the Caseys and intend paying a visit to Sam Hockley. Do you feel like coming for a ride?'

'We sure do. This is a meeting that we would not want to miss. We've been in this since Walter Hill was murdered and want to see this whole mess cleared up at last. Just wait till we get a couple of fresh horses.'

The dogs raised the alarm as they approached Casey's and the rancher and Perez were waiting as they rode up to the house.

Casey looked at the body on the horse. 'Not another one? Who is it?'

Hogan said quietly: 'Relax, Mike. This is a good result. That's Henry Power. The trouble along Warbonnet Creek is just about over. It might be an idea if the women don't see this, though.'

'Too late, Ned,' Jean Casey said. 'I've seen dead people before and so has Ellie. Who killed this man?'

'I did. He was waiting to ambush me on the way back from town. I was lucky, he was packing a leg wound and his rifle got damaged right when he needed it most.'

'So the trouble is all over?' Ellie sounded relieved.

'I'm afraid not, Ellie. I know now who has been sheltering Power and hiding him from us.'

'I knew that Marryat had a hand in this somewhere,' Dave Casey said as he joined the group.

'It wasn't Marryat. It's Sam Hockley. He is only a front for the West Texas Cattle Company who hired Power.'

Casey pushed back his hat and scratched his forehead. 'Well I'll be d—' He caught his wife's glare just in time. 'We spent hours today following Sam all over the place and never found a thing.'

Hogan explained. 'He did that to get you out of the way while Power set an ambush for me.'

Ellie spoke in a tone of disbelief. 'But Sam Hockley seemed such a good man.'

'Well, he ain't,' her father snapped. 'Get the horses,' he told his sons. 'We're going skunk-shooting.'

'Could you get a spare mount for me?' Hogan asked. 'Mine has done a lot of travelling today.'

Jean Casey pointed to the house. 'In there, Ned Hogan, and get something to eat. Another few minutes won't make much difference to Sam Hockley.'

TWENTY

'What's going to happen to Sam?' Ellie asked.

Hogan paused from his eating. 'I don't know. If he surrenders we might have to find an honest lawman to hand him over to. If he makes a fight of it anything can happen.'

'Be careful, Ned.'

'I'll be careful. I have a new ranch house to build and I don't intend to get shot at this late stage of the proceedings. When all this mess is fixed up I'll get you to come over to the Rocking H one day and see where you reckon I should build the new house.'

'And why would my opinion matter so much?' Ellie asked. Although secretly she hoped that she knew the answer.

Casey appeared at the door. 'The horses are ready, Ned.'

'I'll tell you later,' Hogan said as he jumped up from the table.

Ellie glared after the retreating figure of her father. If looks could have killed Mike Casey would at least have suffered serious injury.

Sam Hockley walked to the front door of the ranch house and listened. He had done this several times over the last couple of hours. 'He should be back by now, Wilt. Something's gone wrong.'

Norris poured a bit more whiskey into the tin cup on the table. 'You're worrying too much, Sam. He'll turn up. Fellers like Power have charmed lives. Now stop fussing around like an old lady. Have a drink.'

'I don't want a drink and you should go easy on that stuff too. If those ranchers find out who we really are they'll be gunning for us.'

'Let 'em come,' Norris said. He reached under the table and produced a sawn-off, double-barrelled shotgun. 'I'll turn 'em into wolf bait if they get too big for their boots. But there's no reason they should suspect us even if they get Power. If he's dead, he can't talk and if he's alive he won't talk. The company has a heap of smart lawyers and crooked judges on the payroll. He'll keep his mouth shut and they'll get him out of trouble.'

'They might do that for Power because he knows so much about their operations, but they sure as hell won't do it for us, Wilt. I think something's wrong.'

'Nothing's going to happen this late at night, Sam. Now have a drink and see what happens in the morning.'

'I don't want a drink and you really should lay off it too.'

Hockley paced restlessly to the front of the house and listened again. This time he heard what he did not want to hear. Several riders were approaching. 'There are riders coming. Quick, Wilt, kill that light.'

Norris lurched to his feet and put down his drink. He grabbed a handful of buckshot cartridges from an open box on the table and stuffed them in a pocket. Then he picked up the shotgun and blew out the lamp. 'Let 'em come,' he said in drunken defiance as he made his way to the front door.

Through the front windows, Hockley saw a dark mass of horsemen approaching. As the drunken Norris strode to the front door, he turned and fled out through the back one.

It is doubtful if the man with the shotgun knew of his associate's departure. He threw open the door, stepped onto the veranda and yelled: 'See how you like this, you sheep-herding sonsofbitches.'

He fired both barrels into the approaching

riders. Eighteen large slugs tore into horses or men. Corbett's horse reared straight over backwards. Tom Casey dropped his rifle as he was hit in the upper right arm. Grazed by a slug, Mike Casey's horse began to buck and collided with that of Perez. Suddenly all was confusion with plunging horses and startled riders milling about.

Had Norris waited until his targets were closer, the shots would have been devastating, but round balls fired from smooth bores lost power rapidly after the first thirty yards and wounded rather than killed.

Hogan jumped from his horse, and fired his six-gun at the spot from which the muzzle flashes had come. The gunman was in the deep shadows and was hard to distinguish.

Dave Casey followed Hogan's lead and threw shots into the shadows as quickly as he could work his gun.

Perez too had dismounted and was firing at the gunman on the veranda.

If Norris had been wounded, it did not prevent him from reloading and firing another barrel at the mass of men and horses. Hynes yelled aloud as a couple of pellets hit him in the thigh and others wounded his horse.

By this time Corbett had struggled to his feet and joined Hogan, Perez and Dave Casey in pouring lead at the latest muzzle flash. Suddenly a shape lurched out of the shadows and toppled down the three steps that led to the veranda.

'Got him,' yelled the youngest Casey.

'Be careful,' Hogan warned. 'There are two of them.'

'If there are, there was only one shooting,' Corbett muttered as he punched the empty shells from his gun.

'Is anyone hit?' Mike Casey asked.

'I am,' his son, Tom, told him. 'I'm hit in the arm but I don't think it's broken.'

'I thought I was hit but my chaps must have stopped the slugs,' Hynes announced. 'Thank God we were not ten yards closer.'

Hogan picked up the fallen shotgun, checked it and found one unfired cartridge in it. 'I'm going to search the house in case Hockley's hiding inside. This might come in handy.'

Perez reloaded his gun. 'I'll come with you.'

While Casey went to work on Tom's wounds, Hynes, Corbett, and Dave Casey made a search of the immediate area around the house.

A search of the house proved fruitless and Hogan was just about to start catching and checking the horses for wounds when Corbett called: 'I can hear something over here to my left.'

The others hurried to where the cowhand stood. 'What is it?' Hynes whispered.

'Sounded like somebody moving through long grass. It's stopped now but I reckon he's just lying low.'

'Let's spread out and see what we can scare up,' Hynes suggested.

Hogan warned. 'Be careful. In this bad light we could easily shoot each other. Try to keep in line and only shoot to the front.'

Crouching low in the long grass, Hockley heard the searchers coming slowly closer. He silently cursed the snapped twig that had attracted the hunters to him before he had been able to take full advantage of the opportunity that Norris's drunken courage had given him.

'Sam,' Hogan called. 'Give yourself up. I promise that we'll take you to a proper law officer. There's nothing to be gained by more killing. Give yourself up.'

Hockley stayed quiet. He knew that Hogan was to his left and he had a healthy respect for his shooting ability. Quietly he moved to the right. Progress was painfully slow and he had to wait until the hunters started their advance so that the sound of their movements through the grass would mask his.

The sound of swishing grass came closer.

Against the starlit sky, the silhouette of a man's head appeared. He did not recognize the shape of the hat but knew that it was not Hogan. His options were narrowing. The best he could hope for was that the searcher might not see him. His next best chance would be to shoot the man and run through the gap in the cordon, but without a horse and with his enemies on his heels, Hockley knew that the success of such a plan would be doubtful.

The hunter came closer and the man in the grass knew that he must be discovered.

Hynes was about to withdraw from the search. The heavy chaps had prevented the buckshot from entering his leg but it was badly bruised and was beginning to stiffen. He turned to tell Hogan of his intentions when suddenly he heard a gun being cocked just in front of him. 'Look out!' he shouted as he toppled backwards.

Hockley bounded to his feet, snapped a quick shot at the fallen man and ran past him.

Dave Casey spun and fired his carbine from the hip. The bullet clipped Hockley's shoulder and knocked him off his feet. Corbett, who was next to Casey, ran back and fired at the dark figure on the ground.

Hogan could not fire as Corbett was in the way. But there was no need of further shooting.

Hockley was dead.

'Are you OK?' Casey asked.

'He scared me half to death but missed me,' Hynes explained as he struggled to his feet. 'I reckon I've had all the shooting at me that a man can take in one night.'

The lights were still burning when they returned to Casey's. Jean and Ellie came out with a lantern as the riders dismounted. His mother gave a shriek and ran to where Tom sagged in his saddle.

'It's all right, Jean,' Mike said gently. 'It's nothing serious.'

As soon as she saw that her brother was not seriously injured Ellie hurried to Hogan's side. Ignoring the onlookers she threw her arms about him. 'Is it all over at last, Ned?'

'It's all over, Ellie. We can make plans again.'

'What sort of plans?' she asked softly.

'I was thinking about a new ranch house and a wife to share it with me. Would you be interested?'

She held him tighter. 'What do you think?'